(THE TRILOGY)

By

STACEY COVERSTONE

Enjoy the Journey!

Stacey Coverstone

Lake Tavadora (The Trilogy)

COPYRIGHT © 2015 by Stacey Coverstone

Visit the author's website:
http://www.staceycoverstone.com

Cover Art by Sheri L. McGathy

DEDICATION
To Paul

ACKNOWLEDGEMENTS
Thank you to Anne and Sue for reading and editing this
book. Your generosity of time is much appreciated.

Stacey Coverstone

PART I

JENNIE AND THE LIGHTHOUSE KEEPER

(*The Past*)

CHAPTER ONE

October, 1911
New York Women's Asylum for the Insane

Jennie Sullivan's heart skipped erratically as she stepped through the massive door of the asylum and out into the chilly air. Wearing the same blue skirt and matching jacket that she'd been admitted in twelve months earlier, she tightly clutched the handle of a battered leather suitcase that contained all her worldly possessions.

Standing at the bottom of the steps was Dr. Fitzhugh, the psychiatrist who had made her release possible. His lips lifted in a smile under his bushy mustache, as he waved her forward.

Slowly, Jennie descended the steps, afraid this might be a dream. Since she'd arrived at this hellhole, she'd woken in a sweat to more nightmares than she could count. After the various scientific treatments that had been applied in order to rehabilitate her, her mind felt emptier and her spirit duller. Having been an intelligent, fun loving, and outspoken young woman of nineteen before entering the asylum, it was now difficult to decipher between reality and the quiet world to which she'd withdrawn.

"Come," Dr. Fitzhugh said softly, reaching out his hand. "My driver is waiting for us."

Jennie glanced beyond the doctor to the man standing next to a Model T Ford idling in the gravel driveway. Another figure appeared in her periphery. She turned her head and met the stern gaze of Nurse Talbot, a woman who derived pleasure from tormenting her patients. Jennie inhaled a deep breath and broke the gaze. She would not give Nurse Talbot the satisfaction of acknowledgment.

"Hurry now, Miss Sullivan," Dr. Fitzhugh prodded. "You don't want to miss your train to Florida."

Florida! Jennie's head spun with a combination of excitement and anxiety. So much had transpired in a short time. She was leaving New York and traveling on a train to a small southern town situated on a lake. Both the name of the town and the lake was Tavadora, and what a beautiful image it conjured.

Dr. Fitzhugh's driver stepped forward and nodded hello. Then he reached for her suitcase.

"I'll keep it with me, thank you." She wrapped her hands around the case and pressed it close to her chest. Catching the psychiatrist's eye, she hoped she hadn't spoken out of turn. "That is, if it's all right with you, Doctor."

"Certainly," he replied. He touched her shoulder, and his gaze lit with sympathy. "You're free now, Miss Sullivan. There are no more rules to follow, except those of your conscience. You may do as your heart pleases."

It seemed hard to believe that she was leaving this place for good, but Dr. Fitzhugh had never lied to her. He'd always been kind, despite the treatments he'd ordered.

Before stepping into the Model T, she turned and took one more look at the three-story Gothic monstrosity with turrets and gables that had imprisoned her for twelve long months. Never again would she peer through bars on windows. No longer would she have to cover her ears to drown out the screams and moans of mentally sick women. She would try her best to put the mistreatment she'd suffered behind her. It wouldn't be easy, but her sister Emma would help.

Jennie turned her back on the asylum once and for all and climbed into the vehicle. Dr. Fitzhugh settled his bulk next to her. His driver closed the door, stepped into the driver's seat, and put the car in gear.

Placing the suitcase on her lap, Jennie stared straight ahead, not glancing at the gates that had locked her in as they drove through. Instead, she focused on the dirt road that led toward her new life.

****

When she disembarked the train two days later, a blast of moist heat hit her like a furnace. Perspiration immediately beaded on her brow. Inside her skirt and jacket, her body felt hot and damp. The few pieces of clothing she still owned would never do in this tropical climate. She peered into the cobalt blue sky and let her gaze trail across the tops of palm trees, feeling like she'd landed in another world.

Gripping the suitcase handle, Jennie stepped onto the station platform and glanced around the sea of passengers looking for Emma. She wasn't sure she'd even recognize her sister. She'd only been five years old when Emma married Bill Merrill at eighteen and left New York to move to Florida. She'd be thirty-three now. Although blood relatives, they were strangers.

Despite their estrangement, when Doctor Fitzhugh sent a letter to Emma, she had written back with an enthusiastic offer to take in her younger sibling, as long as someone would pay for Jennie's train ticket. As she'd explained, she and her husband managed a 10-room inn called the Lake House, but they were barely making ends meet, and they had three young children to feed. She hoped he'd understand.

Jennie was ever so grateful that the psychiatrist had been accommodating and purchased her a one-way ticket, since she had no money of her own and no other relatives to rely upon. She and Emma's parents had died in recent years—Father due to a hunting accident and Mother of pneumonia.

As the crowd thinned, her pulse began to throb. Where was Emma? Had she changed her mind about taking her in? Her gaze lifted to the palm trees lining the street, and a floral scent tickled her nose, helping to calm her.

"Can I help you, miss?" Her head swiveled toward the voice. A man in the ticket booth smiled. "You look lost," he said.

"Do you know Emma and Bill Merrill?" she asked. "I was told they work at the Lake House."

The man's smile grew, and he pointed over her shoulder. "The hotel is right over yonder. You should find Mrs. Merrill at the front desk. But if you're looking for Bill, he's most likely sitting on a stool in the local tavern. That's where he tends to spend most of his time."

Jennie frowned. Was her brother-in-law a drunkard? "Thank you," she said and began the short walk to the inn.

The building was three stories, whitewashed with green shutters at all the windows. A covered veranda stretched across the front, where several rocking chairs and potted plants welcomed visitors. When she reached the front steps, her gaze shifted to the grounds in front of the hotel. Different types of citrus, palms, cactus, and other exotic plantings caused her to feel like she'd wandered into a tropical paradise. A walkway led to a sandy beach and to the lake she'd been dreaming about and was anxious to see. Undoubtedly, the proximity of water had inspired the inn's name.

Feeling tears prick her eyes at the beauty surrounding her, Jennie considered pinching her arm to be sure this was real. While locked in her dingy room without a window at the asylum, she'd imagined she would die in that horrid place, alone and feeling there was no justice in the world.

Then a miracle had occurred and she'd been set free. She had a family again. Without further hesitation, she marched up the steps, but stopped before grasping the doorknob. A frightening thought suddenly skittered through her. What if Emma wasn't as welcoming as she appeared in her letters? Jennie didn't know her. Once they'd left New York, Emma and her husband had never returned, not even to attend the funeral of Father and Mother.

What exactly had Dr. Fitzhugh told her about Jennie's incarceration in the mental institution? Did she know about the ice baths and shock therapy? Jennie hadn't asked and the doctor hadn't said. What if Emma knew nothing about the incident that had gotten Jennie locked up? How would her sister treat her when she learned the truth?

Before she had time to ponder further, the door swung open and a tow-haired boy of about ten crashed through, nearly knocking the suitcase out of her hand.

"Sorry, lady!" he hollered before charging past her and down the steps.

The clicking of heels across a wooden floor inside caused Jennie to look up.

"Bill Junior, you come back here right now and apologize to the—" The woman's words halted in mid-sentence when her gaze caught Jennie's. Her eyes enlarged and a hand flew to her mouth.

Paralyzed, Jennie stared at her sister. She'd never seen a picture of her, but Emma was the spitting image of their mother with her white-blond hair and blue eyes.

Emma's hand dropped from her mouth and she inched closer. "Jennie Sullivan? Is it you?"

Unexpected tears spilled from Jennie's eyes and slid down her cheeks. So overwhelmed with emotion, all she could do was nod. When Emma approached and threw her arms around her, Jennie gave in to heaving sobs. The anguish and uncertainty of the past twelve months had built to a breaking point, but her sorrow magically disappeared within her sister's warm embrace.

They held each other for what seemed like an eternity. When they finally parted, Emma stood at arm's length and searched Jennie's face. Then she threaded her fingers through her thick auburn hair. "You look like Father."

"And you look just like Mother," Jennie said, choking back emotion.

Emma's face flushed. "Thank you for the compliment, but I'm not nearly as pretty as her."

Upon closer inspection, Jennie saw dark rings under her sister's eyes. Her teeth needed dental work, and her body was too thin. The Florida heat probably melted off the pounds, and hard work and children could have made her look older than her age.

"Was that your son who ran out the door?" she asked.

"Yes, his name is William, after my husband. We call him Bill Junior. He's ten. David is eight, and my little princess, Becky, turns five soon."

"You're very lucky. What a wonderful family you must have."

"You'll meet them all soon. Come in." Emma led her through the door.

Jennie's gaze perused the lobby with its gleaming hardwood floors, elegant furniture covered in rich brocade fabrics, and potted ferns. Sunlight streamed through the huge plate glass windows that offered a gorgeous view of the grounds and the lake beyond. "And to manage such a beautiful hotel must be like living in heaven."

Her memory snapped back to the asylum with its dark and gloomy interior where not a ray of light or hope had ever shone through.

"It's a lot of hard work is what it is—supervising the cooking and cleaning, helping to make the beds and do laundry, tending to persnickety guests—"

Jennie interjected, "I'm a hard worker. I'll earn my keep." She wanted her sister to know she didn't expect a handout and wouldn't take advantage of her generosity.

Suddenly, Emma's mouth snapped closed and she nibbled her lip, looking embarrassed. Perhaps she realized her complaints were nothing compared to what Jennie had endured at the institution. "We'll talk about all that another day. You must be exhausted after your long trip, and hungry. Would you like something to eat and drink, or do you just want to lie down and rest?"

"I would love some tea with cream and sugar, if it's not too much trouble." It had been so long since Jennie had savored sugar, as sweets weren't allowed at the asylum, but immediately, she felt guilty. All remnants of humanity had been stripped from the patients, making them feel like they didn't deserve something as simple as a nice cup of tea.

"It's no trouble at all," Emma replied kindly. "I'll warm up some biscuits with jam, too, if you'd like. They were made fresh this morning." She smiled and patted Jennie's arm. It was obvious she was trying to make her feel at ease.

"I'd like that very much." On cue, her stomach grumbled.

"Wonderful. I'll take you to your room and then I'll bring up the tea and biscuits."

When Emma reached to pick up Jennie's suitcase, she snatched it out of her hands. Possessive of the few things she could call hers, including her sketchpad and charcoal pencils, she said, "Thank you, but I can carry it."

For a split second, a mixture of confusion and annoyance crossed Emma's face, but she recovered well. "I'm sorry. It's a habit. I'm so used to carrying our guests' luggage to their rooms."

"Doesn't your husband help with that?"

"He does when he's around." Emma changed the subject quickly. "Is this your only piece of luggage?"

Jennie nodded and followed her sister up the stairs to the second floor and down a carpeted hall. Emma unlocked the door to a room in the corner. When Jennie entered, she stood in stunned silence.

The bed was a four poster with a canopy and mosquito netting draped down the sides. An oak desk and chair sat against one wall, a matching bureau on the other. A chaise lounge bedecked in a wine colored fabric jutted from one corner with several books setting on a small table beside it. Large windows afforded a view of the lake and of a small island in the distance. She hadn't noticed the island from ground level, but the sight of it now caused a thrill to spiral up her spine. The scene was postcard perfect and the room so beautiful that she was again flooded with emotion. "Thank you for taking me in!" she exclaimed.

Tears leaked from Emma's eyes. "It's the least I can do for my little sister." She paused. "I'm sorry I wasn't there to help when you really needed me."

What had Dr. Fitzhugh told her? "Do you know why I was committed to the asylum?" Jennie tentatively asked.

Emma shook her head. "The doctor didn't offer information and I didn't ask. All that matters is that you're here now, and we're together."

Overwhelmed by Emma's compassion, Jennie's heart slammed against her rib cage. "Aren't you the least bit curious?" She would be if the roles had been reversed.

"I don't care," Emma stated. "If you want to tell me someday, I'll listen, but I'll not pry. It's not my way."

"You have children. Don't you worry that I could be… dangerous?"

Emma hesitated for the briefest moment. "If your doctor thought you were a danger to me or my

11

family, he wouldn't have released you or contacted me. Would he?"

Her point was valid. Jennie let out the breath she held. "I don't suppose so."

Emma smiled. "There's a pitcher of water and a basin on the bureau. Freshen up and change clothes if you'd like, and I'll be up soon with the tea and biscuits. Here's your room key." She handed Jennie a brass skeleton key.

She clutched the key tightly in her fist. It had been one full year since she'd been in control of who came and went from her room.

Perhaps sensing the importance of the moment, Emma grasped her hand and squeezed it before stepping out and closing the door behind her.

CHAPTER TWO

Being the center of attention was unnerving. Nevertheless, Jennie politely indulged the hotel staff as they treated her like a queen at dinner that night. The Merrill children, too, were fascinated with her. They seemed excited to have a new aunt. Becky especially took to her, showing Jennie her doll and wanting to hold her hand.

The family sat in the dining room at a table draped with white linens. Sweet-smelling candles flickered from brass candlesticks. A young woman with curly red hair cheerfully served them with a friendly smile, and the chef created a dessert in Jennie's honor and delivered it to their table himself.

"We usually eat upstairs in our quarters on the third floor," Emma explained, "but tonight is special, with it being your first night with us."

Jennie flushed with embarrassment. "You needn't have gone to such trouble, but it's all so very nice. I very much appreciate it. The food was wonderful."

Dessert had just been served—Cherries Jubilee—when the bell at the front desk tinkled. Emma scooted out from the table and jumped up. "That must be a guest checking in. I'll be right back."

After having worked all day, planned a nice supper, got her children washed and dressed, as well as helping to make Jennie feel comfortable in her new home, Emma appeared to be run ragged. Jennie glanced at her brother-in-law, wondering why he didn't offer to take care of the guests. His head dropped to his plate, and he shoveled the dessert into his mouth without a glance toward the main lobby.

Bill had grunted a hello upon meeting and then stared at her throughout the meal. He smelled of whiskey, so the ticket master at the train depot had spoken the truth. Poor Emma. Jennie wondered if Bill had been a drinker when her sister married him. Jennie knew he was past forty, but with a full head of wavy brown hair and piercing green eyes, he was still a handsome man. Growing up, she'd only heard Emma's name uttered a few times in her parents' home. Theirs had been a relationship at odds, probably because Emma had run off with a man her parents had thought too old for her.

Bill Junior and David raucously chattered while Becky kept tugging on Jennie's skirt and staring at her through big round eyes. Since Bill didn't respond to any of them, Jennie felt obligated to give them her full attention. She didn't know how to properly interact with adults anymore, let alone children, but she did her best.

With other guests laughing and talking at nearby tables and the redheaded server making a clatter while removing dishes, she began to feel lightheaded. The deluge of noise caused an overload of her senses. Eating at the asylum had been a silent affair—no speaking allowed. When a patient became agitated and made a scene, she was immediately escorted from the dining hall.

Jennie felt a flutter in her chest, and her nerves began to twang. Just when she thought she might faint from anxiety, Emma was at her side, concern etched on her face.

"Are you all right, dear? You look flushed."

"I'm just a little warm," she fibbed. "I think the excitement of the day has caught up with me."

Emma addressed Bill. "I'll take the children upstairs and put them to bed. Will you walk my sister outside so she can get some fresh air?"

When Bill's gaze connected with Jennie's, a shudder ran the length of her. There was nothing particularly sinister about the way he looked at her, but a little voice inside her head issued a warning. She spoke up, albeit softly. "You can finish your dessert, Bill. I can find my way outdoors. I'll walk around the grounds a bit, and perhaps go down and look at the lake."

"Nonsense," Emma said. "It's growing dark and you don't know your way around. You don't want to step on a snake."

"You have snakes?"

"There are all kinds of creatures here that you need to be mindful of. Bill keeps a pistol loaded for such an encounter. He'll be happy to walk to the lake with you. Won't you, Bill?"

"Sure." Suddenly, he seemed interested, and his gaze lingered longer than needed.

"We're all family now," Emma said, smiling. "There's no time like the present for the two of you to get acquainted. Come on, children. You've had enough fun for one day. It's time for bed." She wiped their faces and shooed the children out of their chairs, and the four of them disappeared around the corner, exchanging lively conversation. Jennie heard their footsteps as they trampled up the stairs.

Bill pushed away from the table and lifted a pack of cigarettes from his shirt pocket. "I'm done. Let's go."

Jennie inhaled a breath. "Thank you, but I really think I can find my way to the lake. I don't want to inconvenience you. In fact, I wouldn't mind a few minutes of quiet time before I retire."

He squinted, and his lip curved into a sly grin. "Don't suppose there were many quiet times to be had in the loony bin."

Two people walking past them jerked their heads in their direction at his comment. Jennie felt her face grow hot. Mortified, she bolted from her chair and scurried into the lobby and out the front door, hoping Bill would stay behind. Heavy footfalls caught up with her just as she started down the path toward the lake. He gripped her shoulder and swung her around.

A tiny scream rose in her throat. "Please unhand me," she said, wrenching away. A stew of unwanted memories stirred within her. She'd been manhandled by Nurse Talbot and treated roughly by other attendants. She intended never to let anyone touch her that way again.

Unfortunately, however, her temperament wasn't the same as before. Her resolve was not as strong as it once had been. At the asylum, force and inhumane treatments were used to weaken a person. It had certainly worked on her. She felt her courage crumble under Bill's intense stare.

He took a dramatic step back. "No need to be rude, little sister." He chuckled and lit his cigarette. When he blew a puff of smoke that drifted into her face, she wrinkled her nose and coughed. What kind of a brute had her sister married? Wishing he would leave her alone, she turned and walked briskly toward the shore. Once she reached the water's edge, she craned her head over her shoulder. Seeing no sign of him, she breathed a sigh of relief.

The moon was rising over the water, its pale face round and ethereal. Birds warbled in the nearby trees and something—maybe a fish—splashed near her feet. She jumped back, wondering if there could be alligators in the lake.

The wooden dock looked sturdy, so she stepped onto it and strolled the fifteen or so feet to the end. The evening air was still warm, despite a slight breeze that stirred, and the lake was calm and the setting so serene. She could hardly believe she was in Florida and had reconnected with the sister she never knew. A sense of peace settled over her, and she thought maybe...just maybe in time, she'd be able to put the past twelve nightmarish months behind her.

Lake Tavadora (The Trilogy)

As she meditated on that positive thought, her gaze swept across the water to the small island beyond. Her eyes widened when her gaze fell upon a lighthouse. A rush of adrenaline surged through her body. She'd been entranced by lighthouses ever since a school friend had returned from a journey to Maine wherein she'd described the structures as both magical and eerie. For some unknown reason, Jennie's heart ricocheted in her chest.

From this distance, the lighthouse looked very tall and appeared to be painted one solid color—perhaps red. She could just make out the outline of what was probably the keeper's cottage sitting next to it. Her gaze ran up the base to stop at the gallery deck and then moved on to the lantern room and the cupola on top. A fairy story began to develop in her mind of a maiden with long hair, captured in the tower by an evil king, and the fair-haired hero who climbed the sides in order to rescue her. So deep into the dream was she that she failed to hear footsteps behind her.

Hands at her waist caused her to jolt and nearly lose her balance. She uttered a sharp cry. Spinning and teetering on her heels, the smell of whiskey puffed across her face. Bill laughed and stood her upright like he was setting a pole in the ground.

"Did I scare you?" he drawled, leaving his hands on her waist the way only a husband should touch his wife. He gave her a suggestive squeeze.

She wriggled out of his grasp. "Stop it, Bill!"

"Stop what?"

"Touch me again and I'll...I'll..."

"Touch you? Why, sister, whatever do you mean?"

"Don't call me that. I'm not your sister." For a moment the old, outspoken Jennie surfaced.

"Very well. For someone insane, you're a spunky one, aren't you?"

Jennie felt her tenacity sputter out like a doused flame. "I'm not insane," she mumbled. And she certainly didn't feel spunky. Her breath released in a jagged shudder. Nerves made her next words bite. "I think you should go back to the inn and help Emma with the children, or the guests, or whatever she needs help with. She looks very tired tonight."

His eyes narrowed. "Emma doesn't need my help. She's independent. She doesn't need a man for anything." His dark glare caused the hair on Jennie's scalp to prickle. "Twelve months is a long time to be locked away," he continued, angling his head. "What a shame. I'll bet a pretty young thing like you got lonely..." His words trailed off. Sweat glowed across his upper lip, and he shifted his body closer.

Foreboding rose like the tide. With a burst of energy, she gave him a shove and sprang past him to run up the dock as fast as her feet would carry her. When she reached the walk, she glanced quickly over her shoulder and saw his figure still at the end of the pier. She heard the strike of a match cut through the silent air. The red spark of Bill's cigarette lit up the dark. She hastened to the inn and up the front steps with her heart pounding.

Emma was at the front desk when she entered the lobby, trembling and out of breath.

"Jennie, dearest, are you all right?" Emma rushed from behind the desk and placed her palm at her cheek. "You're pale. Have you seen one of our ghosts that prowl the grounds?"

"Ghosts?" Jennie felt her eyes enlarge.

Emma chuckled and put her arm around her. "I'm just joking. What happened? Did something frighten you?"

"I...I thought I saw one of those snakes you mentioned," she fibbed.

"Oh. They're not poisonous, but they do give one a fright when you're not expecting them. Did you go down to the lake? It's so pretty this time of evening."

Jennie nodded, fretting over whether she should inform her sister of Bill's advances and boorish behavior. *Were* they advances, or had he only been teasing her? Unsure of her own ability to determine the difference, her brain felt cloudy.

As if reading her mind, Emma said, "Did you and Bill have a nice chat?"

A chat was not what she would have called it, but Emma was the only family Jennie had. Bill had not behaved in a way one would consider brotherly, but she couldn't lose her sister over what was probably a misunderstanding on her part. She had nowhere else to go. "Yes," she answered simply. "But I'm quite tired now. Do you mind if I go to bed?"

"Of course I don't mind, dearest. It's been a long day full of changes. If you need anything at all, our suite is on the third floor. Don't hesitate to knock." She kissed her cheek. "I'm glad you're here."

Jennie grabbed her sister's hands, feeling warmth flood her body. "I don't know how I'll ever be able to repay you for your generosity."

"There's no need. We're family." She smiled. "Sleep well, and I'll see you in the morning."

Before she burst into grateful tears, Jennie rushed up the stairs and entered her room, locking the door behind her.

She thought she'd fall into bed and immediately drop off to sleep, but as soon as she changed into her night dress, her mind began to race. Overwhelming hardly seemed a strong enough word to describe the sudden changes in her life. She pulled back the drapes and stood at the window gazing upon the grounds below, hoping to clear her mind.

A blanket of stars dotted a sky that was darker than ink. Beyond the grove of plants, Lake Tavadora was barely visible. The only light came from the gossamer shimmer cast by the moon upon the water. The gleaming luminosity of the southern moon was lovelier than she could have imagined.

Jennie yawned. Just as she was about to close the drapes, another radiant light caught her attention. As if a switch had been turned on, a narrow beam shone out from what could only be the lighthouse across the lake. It seemed to be pointing straight at her. Frozen, she barely breathed as it pulsed once…twice…three times, and then abruptly went out.

A few moments passed with her staring into a sea of darkness.

With her heart beating fast, a spark started at her wrists and flickered through her body to light her insides. "Perhaps I'll borrow a rowboat from someone and go to that little island and explore the lighthouse one of these days."

The notion came out of the blue, and she grinned. The feeling was strange. It had been so long since she'd had anything to smile about, but the image of being on her own and doing what she pleased—just as Doctor Fitzhugh had promised—caused hope to spring into her breast.

CHAPTER THREE

The next few weeks flew by. Jennie helped Emma at the inn, doing everything from laundry to making beds to babysitting her niece and nephews, whom she grew close to quickly. It felt good to contribute and belong to the world again. Emma even paid her. The recompense was meager, but it was something—and it was a start, a new beginning.

Her confidence had been building, too. The nightmares were coming fewer and farther between. Memories of what had been done to her in the asylum were starting to fade. Each day, she'd steal a few moments and go somewhere different to sit and draw. Drawing had been her saving grace at the institution. Not that she'd had much inspiration in that lonely, depressing place. But here, she could sketch the magnificent flowers, citrus, and tropical plants and trees, as well as the lake that whispered her name.

It would take a little more time, but Jennie was beginning to feel like her old self again.

One incident in particular helped her self-assurance to grow. She'd been cleaning a guest room and bending over to sweep dust from under the bed with a broom when the door clicked closed behind her. Bill had rushed forward, stinking of whiskey. He'd gripped her waist with both hands and said, "My, my, this is too tempting to resist."

She let out a screech. "Bill, let me go!"

"What will you do if I don't?" he challenged.

She balled her fist and punched his arm, which only made him laugh. "I'll tell Emma that you're a philanderer," she threatened. Besides her own encounters with him, one of the housekeepers, a busy body who enjoyed sharing gossip, had told her stories about Bill's escapades with drink and other women. Poor Emma deserved to know that she was married to a dirty old goat, but perhaps she *did* know and turned a blind eye because of the children.

"You wouldn't tell your sister," he said. "She's your only kin and you need her. Anyway, who do you think she'll believe? Her husband, or a crazy girl she hasn't seen in fifteen years?"

"I will, so help me," Jennie warned.

He jerked her closer. "Ooh, Jennie, you are packed nicely. How about a little tussle? I know it's been at least a year for you."

She'd never been with a man before, and she wasn't about to start with him. "Get your hands off me, Bill!" She kicked his shin. He grunted but didn't let go.

He stuck his nose in her neck and breathed deeply. "You want to know something, Jennie? There's more fire in you than your sister has shown in fifteen years. I deserve a little amusement. Why don't we climb onto this bed and make the springs squeak?"

The blood boiled in her veins. He was the most despicable man on earth. When he slid his hand up her calf, she kneed him in the groin.

Bill howled and let loose. For good measure, she whacked him upside the head with the broom before running from the room. Once she'd made it to safety downstairs, she chuckled at the memory of his blustery face.

Since that incident, her brother-in-law had steered clear of her, for the most part. He still stared at her, and he occasionally brushed against her when Emma wasn't looking. When he did, however, she elbowed him hard in the ribs.

Every night, when she was ready to retire, Jennie stood at the window in her room and glanced at the clock on the bureau. Without fail, the beam shone from the lighthouse at the same time. One…two…three pulses and then it was gone.

With giddiness spreading through her like the scent of orange blossoms, she slipped into bed each night dreaming of the day she would visit the island and see the lighthouse up close.

That day came one morning when she noticed a rowboat tied to the dock. After making a few inquiries, she learned that the boat belonged to a fisherman by the name of Jack Butterfield, and he could be found manning the post office. She immediately sought out the man. Having never rowed a boat before, she nevertheless was compelled to inquire as to whether the old, silver-haired fellow wearing a captain's hat would rent the boat to her.

His eyebrow arched. "Rent it to you and not your husband?"

"I'm unmarried."

He petted the Jack Russell dog sitting on a stool beside him. Then his piercing blue eyes narrowed in curiosity. "Where do you wish to go in my boat?"

Warmth pooled in the pit of her stomach at saying the words out loud. "Across the lake. I'm very interested in exploring the island and the lighthouse."

"The lighthouse, you say? No one lives there anymore, you know."

She didn't know, as she hadn't mentioned a word to anyone—not even Emma—about the pulsing beam that seemed to be speaking to her and her obsessive need to answer.

"It's been abandoned for years," he stated.

She tilted her head in confusion. If it was abandoned, how was the light continuing to shine each night? A reasonable solution came to her quickly. Perhaps no one lived there anymore, but a keeper probably still tended to the light and lens each evening.

"Have you ever rowed a boat before?" Mr. Butterfield asked, interrupting her musings. "It's not an easy task, and I dare say it's not a proper undertaking for a lady."

Her heart dropped. He wasn't going to rent her the boat. Disappointment must have flattened her face, because when her gaze flew to the ground, he chirped up. "I suppose it wouldn't hurt for me to give you a quick lesson. The lake ain't all that big, and you look stout enough to handle the job."

Jennie didn't mind being called stout at all. She wanted to hug the man!

They agreed to meet at the dock right after lunch. Mr. Butterfield would show her how to handle the rowboat and then she could take it out. "For the next couple of weeks," he explained, "I'm helping here at the post office while the postmistress is out of town. Butch and I won't need the boat back until closing time at five o'clock."

"Who is Butch?" Jennie inquired.

"My little buddy." He pointed to the cute dog wagging its tail.

"Oh." She smiled and patted Butch on the head. Although he sported two elongated scars, one on each cheek, he seemed healthy and happy. "I won't be that long," she assured. "Two or three hours at the most."

Fortunately, Emma didn't ask questions when Jennie returned to the inn and asked if she minded her being away for a few hours that afternoon. "I should be back by three o'clock."

"You're a grown woman," Emma said. "You don't need my permission when you want to take time for yourself. I'll get by without you for a few hours."

Her sister had been wonderful about encouraging her to create her art and to explore the town and meet people. "Thank you, Emma!" She could barely control her enthusiasm as she trotted up the stairs to collect her supplies from her room.

****

She listened carefully to Mr. Butterfield's instruction. Once he was confident she could handle the rowboat, including how to dock and anchor it on the other side, he helped her in. The satchel holding her sketchbook and pencils hung securely over her shoulder. She settled on the wooden bench, set the satchel beside her, and took up the oars.

"Oh! In my excitement I almost forgot to pay." She dug her fingers into the pocket of her dress for coins. "How much do I owe you?"

Mr. Butterfield swept his hand through the air. "Save your money, miss. Have yourself a fine day. And don't forget what I taught you."

"I won't. Thank you, Mr. Butterfield."

"One more thing," he said. "There are gators in the lake. You aren't afraid of gators, are you?"

Butch, who had been sitting on the shore watching the whole time, barked and began dancing in a circle.

She gulped. Who wouldn't be afraid of alligators? But if she confessed to being fearful, Mr. Butterfield would probably rethink his liability and change his mind about letting her use the boat.

"I'm not afraid."

The old man smiled. "Good. In that case, if you see a fella about ten feet long that looks older than Methuselah, just say howdy and keep on rowing. He won't bother you."

Ten feet long?

28

He pushed the boat into the water before she could respond, and all thoughts of reptiles flew from her head.

"Bye bye," he called, waving.

"I'm doing it, I'm doing it," she repeated, the mantra keeping time with her strokes. With no breeze stirring, the wooden oars sliced through the cerulean water with ease. Although the lake was not large, her heart fluttered in her chest as the distance between her and Tavadora broadened. Her shoulders were rigid with tension. Training her eye on the hotel sitting on the hill, as well as counting strokes out loud kept her panic in check. Before long, however, her body began to relax and she started to enjoy the adventure.

A short time later, the boat skimmed through tall grass and thudded onto sand. A couple of Great White Egrets jutted their long necks out, picking damselflies out of the air, unfazed by her intrusion.

On wobbly legs, Jennie stood. She'd done it! She'd rowed herself across the lake.

Slinging her satchel over her shoulder, she stepped onto shore, careful not to snag her shoe on the hem of her dress. In short time, she'd anchored the boat the way Mr. Butterfield had instructed. Too energized by the extraordinary feat she'd just accomplished, she barely noticed the water sloshing into her shoes. The air hardly stirred. There was no noise except for the buzz of insects and the quiet sounds made by the egrets. She felt totally alone, but she wasn't afraid.

Her gaze lifted and there it stood, poking up from behind trees and scruffy bushes—the lighthouse.

Without wasting a moment, she trudged through the sand. With her pulse throbbing in her neck and wrists, she ignored the gnats flying around her face and pressed through the bushes. When the land opened up, a path of withered grass led her to the foot of the lighthouse. Next to it sat the keeper's cottage. Staring in awe, her gaze moved up and down the tall structure. The magnetic pull she'd been feeling for the past several weeks was stronger than ever.

Almost reverently, Jennie stepped toward it and placed her hand on the base. The red paint was chipped from weather and erosion, but the concrete felt warm to the touch. Her lips lifted in a smile as her gaze landed on the small wooden door—the entrance to the magical place she'd been imagining. She put her hand on the doorknob, anxious to peek inside, but disappointingly, it was locked.

Her breath escaped through her mouth in short puffs.

After allowing herself a moment of disappointment, she said, "That's all right."

She hadn't intended on traversing the stairs anyway, especially if they were winding, as she was afraid of heights. She'd simply wanted to take a look inside since she'd been picturing the interior for what seemed like a long time.

Since that was impossible, she strolled to the keeper's house and peered through the dirty front windows. The inside was dark, but a tremor ran through her as her gaze shifted around the room. Mr. Butterfield had said the place was abandoned, so she hadn't expected to find furniture inside, including a rocker and a couch. The pieces didn't look in such bad shape from this vantage point. In fact, there was an open newspaper lying on a foot stool in front of a brick hearth. A bottle of beer and a plate of what looked like cheese and crackers sat on the wooden kitchen table.

Odd. Probably some children had been playing in the house, or a fisherman had recently used the cottage for a camp-out.

Suddenly, a chill washed over Jennie. It felt as if eyes were on her. Was she alone? Could she be in danger? A flock of Herring Gulls squawked above her, giving her a fright.

"Don't be silly," she said aloud. "The sun is shining, it's a lovely afternoon, and there's nothing to be afraid of. There's no one else on this island."

She opened her satchel and removed the towel she'd brought to sit on and laid it upon the dry grass in front of the lighthouse. Realizing her shoes were waterlogged, she pulled them off and rubbed her wet feet with the bottom of her dress. Then she took out her sketchpad and charcoal pencils and began to draw the majestic tower looming above her.

CHAPTER FOUR

Sometime later when the sketch was finished, Jennie lay on her back and stared at the cottony clouds floating through the azure sky. Before long, her eyes grew heavy and she curled her fist under her head to use as a pillow.

She must have fallen asleep, because the jiggle of her arm woke her. Unsure as to whether she was dreaming, she lazily opened her eyes.

"Hello." The deep, masculine voice was like liquid caramel, oozy and delicious. A man knelt at her side.

Jennie's eyes popped open and she jolted to an upright position. Though her first response was to run, she was paralyzed by fear. It was virtually impossible to speak or move her limbs.

He stood quickly and took several steps back. "I didn't mean to frighten you. Don't be scared. I won't hurt you."

For some unknown reason, she believed him.

The sun must have been beating down on her for…how long had she been asleep? Jennie felt hot, and perspiration dripped between her breasts inside her dress. Mustering all the strength she had, she stumbled to her feet. Her hand went to her hair that had fallen out of its knot at the back of her head; her curls rested on her shoulders. Her dress was wrinkled and her feet were bare. This was not the way a lady presented herself in front of a man.

"I…I…," she stuttered.

He smiled. "There's no need to explain anything to me, miss. I understand."

Jennie searched his face, and then her gaze subtly skimmed over the rest of him. She had the most peculiar sensation, as if something inside her recognized him. He possessed everything she'd dreamed of in her childhood fantasies—wide shoulders that tapered to a trim waist, fair hair and ocean-blue eyes that pierced through her defenses. She'd heard of love at first sight, but as she held this man's gaze, she could almost believe in it.

"What do you understand, sir?" she asked, her voice unsure.

"That you were creating an artistic rendering of the lighthouse and the warm weather made you sleepy." He grinned again, showing a row of even teeth. "I must confess I took a gander at your sketchbook before I woke you. You're a very fine artist. I'm quite impressed with your talent."

She stared at the sketch on the ground. No one had ever told her she was a fine artist or that she had talent—not even her parents. Her father had even complained that art was a waste of time.

"Thank you, sir, for the kind compliment."

"You're welcome." He tipped his head and said, "I'm sorry to have interrupted you. I'll leave you to your work. Good day."

"Wait!" He wasn't leaving, was he? She couldn't let him go just yet. The need to know something about him drove her to boldly speak up.

"Yes?"

Gulping back a dry throat, she curtsied and said, "Pleased to meet you. My name is Jennie Sullivan. I live in Tavadora at the Lake House." She pointed in that direction. "My sister and her husband manage the hotel."

He strode forward. To her surprise, he reached for her hand and clasped it between his two firm palms. When he kissed her knuckles, she nearly swooned. "The pleasure is mine, Miss Sullivan."

Heat flashed up her neck and crept into her cheeks. How she wished she were more presentable, although he didn't seem to care one iota about her disheveled appearance. "Are you the keeper of the lighthouse?" she asked.

For a moment, a blank expression filled his face. Then he coughed and said, "Yes, yes, I am."

"I thought so! I watch the beam from my window on the second floor of the inn every night. The light has beckoned to me."

"It has?" His gaze shifted from the bottom of the structure to the top and held for a moment. Then his head turned, and he stared at her with playful intensity.

She felt her face flush. He might think her a silly goose for such a fanciful notion.

"I've wanted to come over and explore this island and the lighthouse for weeks," she continued.

"An old man let me borrow his rowboat today so I could finally make the trip." It was hard to contain her zeal, knowing this handsome man tended the light. She hadn't talked this much since before being admitted to the asylum and realized she was chattering like a jaybird. "I'm sorry. I'm talking too much."

When he chuckled, his bright eyes sparkled. "No, you're not. I love your enthusiasm and the way you wave your hands around when you speak."

It was true, when she was nervous, she did talk with her hands.

"Did you say you rowed a boat across the lake by yourself?" he inquired.

"Yes."

His brow arched.

Was he equally impressed with that achievement as he claimed to be about her art? Or was he appalled by her behavior that was less than ladylike? The few seconds that he made her wait before reacting were torture.

Finally, his lips lifted in a crooked smile and he said, "That's quite brave of you, Miss Sullivan. I admire your spunk."

Spunk. It was the second time that word had been used to describe her.

Their gazes latched and Jennie thought she might melt under his gentle scrutiny. She glanced up and down the beach. "Where is *your* boat?"

"Uh, it's being repaired in town. There's a hole in the bottom." He changed the subject quickly. "Would you like a cup of tea?" he asked, gesturing toward the cottage. "Or a bottle of beer?"

The invitation caught her off guard. Never had she been offered beer in her life, and especially not by a man. Although she was old enough for beer, she said, "Tea would be nice."

By this time her shoes had dried out, so she pulled them onto her feet and stuffed the towel and her art supplies into her satchel.

He led her into the small cottage and lit a lamp to illuminate the space. "I apologize for the way the place looks. The maid didn't come today."

When she realized he was joking, she chuckled, and he offered her a seat in the rocking chair.

As he puttered around the small kitchen preparing the tea, Jennie wondered what Emma would say if she knew her sister was alone with a stranger. It was far from appropriate, but she didn't feel ashamed. It felt like she knew this man, or at least his heart.

She glanced around the room, taking in the sparse but masculine furnishings. An open door led to another room—a bedroom. Her breath hitched when her gaze landed on the iron bed in the corner. Abruptly, she averted her eyes.

When the tea was ready, he handed her a cup and she took a sip. "Delicious. You put sugar in it. How did you know I love sweet tea?"

"It was just a hunch."

Jennie smiled, feeling it was more than that.

He scooted the foot stool next to her. "Tell me about yourself, Miss Sullivan."

Oh, my. He seemed to want to know her as much as she wanted to know him.

****

They talked and laughed together for the next hour. But despite how interested she'd initially been in the lighthouse, she didn't think to ask him any questions about his position as the keeper. She remained enthralled by his stories of the sea and sailors from the past.

Before she knew it, the time had come for her to leave. "I promised my sister I'd be back by three," she said, standing up. "I help at the inn with her children and other chores."

"That's good of you." He followed suit and stood as well. "I'll walk you to your boat."

They didn't speak again until they arrived at the water's edge, whereupon he assisted her into the vessel. The heat of his hand touching hers sent ripples through her body. She settled onto the bench and took up the oars, her mood darkening at the thought of not seeing him again.

"Are you sure you're not too tired to row back?" he asked.

"There's no wind, so it should be fast sailing."

He nodded firmly. "I have a feeling you're a mighty fine sailor."

His faith in her abilities made her brighten. Twelve months in the asylum had nearly drained her of her confidence, but day by day, Jennie was becoming the strong person she'd been before.

His next comment made her spirit soar. "I very much enjoyed our time together today, Miss Sullivan, and I wish it was not ending."

"I feel the same way." She surprised herself by blurting, "I could come again. Mr. Butterfield has given me permission to use his rowboat for the next two weeks, and I'm sure my sister won't mind if I take an excursion now and then."

"I would like that very much." His grin was warm and genuine. "Shall we meet here tomorrow at the same time?"

"Yes, we shall."

He shoved the boat into the water, not caring that the bottom of his trousers got wet. "Until tomorrow, Captain Sullivan," he teased, clicking his heels together and saluting her.

"Tomorrow," she chuckled. Once she maneuvered the rowboat onto a straight path, she began rowing. He stood at the shoreline watching as the space between them lengthened. Suddenly, Jennie realized she didn't even know his name. "Sir!" she hollered. "You never told me your name!"

For a moment, it appeared he hadn't heard her. Then he cupped his hands around his mouth and shouted back, "Seth Thacker!"

Pulling in a breath, she released her hand from one of the oars and waved. He waved back, fixing her with a stare so powerful that every nerve tingled with awareness.

By the time she reached the other side of the lake, Jennie was in love.

CHAPTER FIVE

Every afternoon for the next two weeks, Jennie and Seth rendezvoused at the lighthouse. She had never felt so content. With each hour that passed, they grew closer. Discovering they had many things in common, including their fondness for nature and wildlife, as well as fundamental morals and values, they talked about everything under the sun. Everything, that was, except his family. She told him about her parents, Emma, and her niece and nephews. But when she asked Seth about his family, he became close-mouthed and gently switched the subject.

Although she would have liked to know every detail about him, she was surprised to realize that she found Seth's mysterious side most attractive. She didn't begrudge him a small secret. After all, she'd not shared anything about her past incarceration with him. It wasn't because she didn't trust him, because she did, but her past was just that. Those horrible twelve months were now a distant memory, replaced by a joyous present and a possible future with the man of her dreams.

A routine developed. Each day they walked the beach, collecting shells and watching the birds hunt and peck. Seth explained the history of the area and regaled her with humorous stories with local flavor. Sometimes he cooked them a meal and sometimes they cooked together, creating trouble-free dishes from whatever was in the cottage pantry.

They sat on a blanket in the sand in their bare feet and drank beer. She sketched the lake with her charcoal pencils. He stretched out with his hands clasped behind his head, telling jokes, praising her talent, and occasionally touching her arm.

Having been deprived of simple pleasures while in the institution, Jennie reveled in the comfort of a happy and uncomplicated life with a man she loved.

The first time he kissed her, their lips met in a soft, seductive dance. Her body lit like a flame. When she placed her hands upon his cheeks and pulled his face closer, Seth's tongue swept into her mouth with strokes she felt at her core. Gasping at the power of the demand his mouth made, the kiss went on and on until she felt her lips might become bruised.

Finally it ended with both of them breathless and falling into a companionable silence.

****

Love branded a smile on her face, infusing her with a glow. One day, Emma stopped Jennie as she was hurrying to leave the inn for her afternoon row across the lake.

"I think Florida suits you," her sister said.

"I love it here and can never thank you enough for taking me in."

"You don't need to keep thanking me. I did what anyone would do for family." She gave Jennie the once over, smiling slyly. "Where have you been rushing off

41

to every afternoon?" When Jennie nibbled her lip, Emma quickly said, "It's not my place to pry. I apologize for asking."

Inhaling a relieved breath, Jennie ignored Emma's curious gaze. "Is there anything else you need my help with this afternoon?" Tomorrow was Becky's birthday, and she'd been helping Emma with preparations. But she was anxious to see Seth, and gray clouds were starting to gather in the sky. She wanted to cross the lake before it started raining. She'd worry about the return trip later.

"I believe we're set for the party tomorrow," Emma replied. "Enjoy the rest of your day."

"Thank you. I will." And off she went.

As always, Seth waited for her on the shore. He anchored the rowboat and extended his hand toward her. There was no hesitation from either of them by this time. As soon as he assisted her out of the boat, their faces drew together and they kissed.

"I've missed you desperately," he breathed into her hair, hands planted firmly on her arms.

She chuckled lightly. "You just saw me yesterday."

"But that was a very long twenty-four hours ago."

"I missed you, too." Their gazes fused, and she spoke softly. "When I see the beam from the lighthouse each night from my window, I imagine you're thinking of me. When I sleep, you pervade my dreams. And when I wake, your face is the first thing I want to see…"

It was not like her to speak with such frankness, but it felt as if she'd known Seth all her life. There were no barriers between them—no rules of propriety to follow while they were alone on their island.

Seth's face suddenly twisted, and for a moment, she thought she saw pain behind his eyes. Or perhaps it was trepidation. She was in love, but was he? Thinking she'd said too much too soon, she swiftly added, "Which is why I'm going to sketch you today. Then I'll always have your likeness to keep me company."

A slow smile parted his lips, and he glanced into the sky. "A storm is brewing."

"In that case, I'd better get started." She nudged him toward the lighthouse and positioned him in front of the wooden door, where he leaned back and hiked his foot against the base. Then she removed her pencil and sketchpad from her satchel and began to draw. Neither of them talked as she worked.

Just as she finished his portrait, the sky cracked open and rain fell in sheets. Jennie jammed her supplies into the bag, and Seth drew her into the crook of his arm. They ran for the keeper's cottage. When he closed the door securely behind them, she began to shiver in her wet clothes. She hung the satchel on a hook beside the door. Outside the wind started to howl. Rain pounded against the small windows, sounding like shots from a gun, causing her to jump.

Her teeth clinked together when she stuttered, "I...I...hope Mr. Butterfield's rowboat doesn't come l...l...loose and d...drift away."

Seth ran a hand through his wet hair. "Have no fear. I secured it tightly."

"Of course you did." She hugged herself trying to ward off a convulsion of chills racing through her body.

"You're going to catch your death." He strode to the hearth and hastily started a fire with some pieces of timber. When the flames caught, he stood and motioned for her. As if an invisible string pulled her, she glided towards him. When she reached his side, the fire's glow made his features all the more handsome. His passion-filled eyes searched her face, and his hands settled upon her shoulders.

"You can't leave in this storm," he said.

"I know."

"It may last all night."

"That is a possibility."

No more words were spoken, but Jennie understood the language of desire.

When Seth's fingers nimbly unfastened the buttons of her blouse and pulled the fabric apart to expose her skin, she didn't flinch. His eyes widened when he gazed upon her creamy décolletage.

With one fast movement, he scooped her into his arms, carried her through the door of the bedroom, and set her on the bed in the corner. He slipped the shoes off her feet and tossed them on the floor before removing his own. When he swung himself onto the mattress beside her, the springs creaked.

As he began to apologize for the noisy springs, she silenced him with a kiss. "It sounds like a song," she whispered.

And they began to make their own music.

****

Sometime in the night, Jennie woke to realize she was cradled in Seth's arms. Her body was naked but warm. His leg was draped over hers, holding her prisoner, but it was a prison she would gladly endure. Wondering what time it was, a ripple of panic flowed through her at knowing Emma would be worried sick. As if reading her mind, Seth's deep voice cut through her musings.

"Your sister will understand that you chose to stay the night on the island rather than risk a dangerous voyage across the lake in a storm."

"She doesn't know I come here every day."

"At any rate, she will trust you found a safe place to hole up for the night."

Jennie nodded, praying he was right. The certainty in his voice was reassuring, but another thought intruded. "Mr. Butterfield! He probably thinks I sunk his boat. And he may not have had a way to get home."

Seth stroked her cheek. "I'm sure Mr. Butterfield was able to make alternate plans." He smiled and rubbed his hand down her thigh, easing her anxiety.

With her eyes adjusted to the dim light cast from the embers that still glowed in the hearth, Jennie stared into Seth's face. He kissed her lips and then huskily whispered, "I love you, darling."

Delighted that such a handsome and enticing man could reciprocate her feelings, she felt tears burn her eyes. "I love you, too."

Now that they'd said the words, she felt he needed to know the truth about her. She didn't want him to hear about her stint in the asylum from someone else. The way Bill drank, he could get drunk one night and leak her story to whoever was listening. Eventually, it could get back to Seth. "There's something I want to tell you." Her story came out in a rush as she condensed the horrible experience.

"Before coming to Florida, I lived in upstate New York and worked in the home of a very wealthy man as a governess to his two young children. One day I was traversing the back stairs that led from the kitchen to the hallway. I heard cries and caught him abusing an eleven-year-old servant girl." She clenched her fists as the memory resurfaced.

"Fury rose in me like high tide. I held a tray of snacks for his children, which seems so ironic now. My first instinct was that of an animal wanting to attack its enemy. My only weapon was the silver tray, so without thinking, I simply reacted and smashed it over the master's head. With a startled grunt, he whirled. His face was as red as a beet, so angry he was. Before I could escape, he grabbed my throat and began to squeeze. I punched him in the stomach and he let loose, but there was a murderous fire in his eyes. His hands reached out for me again. I had no option but to protect myself, so I smashed him in the face with the tray. And I did so again and again over his head and in the face until he fell to the ground, cut and bleeding."

She stopped to inhale a deep breath. Seth's steady breathing both calmed and worried her, but it was too late to turn back. She continued. "A doctor was called in. The master's injuries to his brain were severe. So severe, in fact, that his wife was told he would never talk or walk again. He would be a vegetable for the rest of his life."

Jennie waited for a response.

Seth's mumbled voice cut through the silence. "He deserved it, but what happened to you?"

"I told the doctor what I'd seen on the stairs. Although it was clear that the master had been attacking that poor little girl—his trousers were still down around his knees when the doctor examined him—and he would have strangled me if I hadn't defended myself, the man was wealthy and I was just the governess. The police were not even called in, and the doctor unilaterally determined me to be insane. I was committed to a women's asylum." There was no need for her to give him the gory details regarding the "treatments" that had been forced on her. "I would have spent the rest of my life in that hellhole had it not been for a kind psychiatrist who rallied for my release and my sister who took me in."

"My poor darling girl," Seth said quietly. He pulled her face close. "What a terrible ordeal you've gone through."

"Do you think different of me?" she asked.

He stared into her eyes. "How could I? You wanted to protect that child, and you had no option but to protect yourself. You were a brave woman." He stroked the top of her head. It was a long time before he spoke again. When he did, he said, "All of that is in the past. It's time for you to seize what the future holds."

She smiled as the vision of a perfect life rolled through her mind.

"Could you imagine yourself living here on this island, with me?" he asked.

Helping him tend the lighthouse? Was he proposing marriage? Before she had time to respond, he grew solemn and shook his head. "I'm sorry, my darling. I spoke out of turn. You deserve more than what I can give."

"But you're all I want."

He stared at her for a long time.

Every nerve in her body flared when he rolled on top of her. The press of his hard muscular form against her breasts and the soft flesh of her belly ignited another firestorm that incinerated everything but her need for him. As they expelled simultaneous groans, the bedsprings began to squeak again.

CHAPTER SIX

The following morning, the birds squawked loudly outside, seeming to extol Jennie's happiness. After tea and toast, she said, "I don't want to go, but I must."

Seth cupped her face in his hands. A fleeting expression of sadness filled his eyes. "I know. Last night was a night I'll always remember."

"As will I." She lifted her satchel off the hook and together they walked to the shore. Thankfully, the rowboat was still anchored. The crisp tang of brine invaded her nose, and the lake rippled with remnants from the storm. As they stood beside the boat, she said, "Today is my niece's birthday. We're having a party this evening."

"That means you won't be back this afternoon." It was a statement, not a question.

"No, but we can still see each other. I would love it if you could attend the party. It begins at five o'clock. I'd very much like you to meet my sister and the children. And my brother-in-law," she added, with a roll of her eyes. She could hardly wait to see Bill's face when she introduced Seth as her intended. Finally, he'd stop pestering her.

Seth stared at her until physiology forced him to blink. An unsettling light kindled in his eyes, and foreboding boomed inside her like thunder. As Jennie waited for his answer, every atom of air left her lungs.

Something strong and hot expanded her heart until she was sure her chest wouldn't hold it.

His hand closed around hers with a gentleness that indicated he would never abuse his strength. "I would love to come to your niece's party. Thank you for the invitation."

The icy thread that had wound its way up her spine melted. "Then I'll see you at five tonight."

"I love you," he said.

"I love you, too, my darling."

They kissed, and then Seth lifted her into the rowboat. As she waved goodbye and the oars began to slice through the water, Jennie felt her heart beat an agonizing staccato—partly from missing him already and partly from the unease that snuck along her ribcage.

****

It was eight o'clock and Seth had still not shown up.

"Is there a way you can contact your friend?" Emma asked, after putting the children to bed. She and Jennie sat in the rockers on the veranda. Becky and the boys were assuredly fast asleep upstairs, worn out from the party. Bill had disappeared sometime after Becky opened her gifts, and one of Emma's employees was manning the front desk, so the sisters were able to spend a few quiet moments together. "Perhaps he got sick or injured himself."

Jennie had considered every possibility. Her nerves were frayed from worry. "The only way of contacting him is to take Mr. Butterfield's rowboat across the lake. But now I've waited too long and it's growing dark."

Emma stopped rocking and stared. "Is that what you've been doing these past couple of weeks? Rowing a boat across the lake?"

"Yes. Mr. Butterfield gave me rowing lessons and loaned me his boat."

Emma's mouth dropped open. "Well, I'll be a monkey's uncle. I had no idea. You really have come a long way since you arrived, haven't you?" She patted Jennie's hand, obviously pleased, and began rocking again.

"That's where Seth and I met. He's the lighthouse keeper."

Emma's rocker halted once more. "What did you say?"

Jennie kept her eyes peeled on the walk leading to the inn from the lake, just in case Seth magically appeared. "My friend. He's the keeper of the lighthouse."

"Jennie, that lighthouse has been abandoned for years. There is no keeper anymore."

"That's what Mr. Butterfield told me, but you both must be wrong. The signal light shines every night at the same time. I watch it from my bedroom window. It's like a secret message from Seth." Despite being concerned for his safety, she smiled, because thinking of him made her so happy.

"Seth? That's your friend's name?"

"Yes." Wasn't Emma listening to a word she said? A flash of annoyance raced through Jennie's veins.

"What's Seth's last name?"

"Thacker." Her neck stretched out upon glimpsing a figure coming from around the corner, but the hope blossoming in her chest faded when the porch lanterns illuminated Bill's face. He strode up the stairs and stopped. Jennie could smell whiskey on him from six feet away.

"Bill!" Emma's voice cracked like a whip.

Jennie turned, surprised at her tone. "What's wrong, Emma?"

Her sister gestured for Bill to approach. "Jennie says her friend, the one who didn't show up tonight, is the lighthouse keeper across the lake and his name is *Seth Thacker*." She emphasized the name.

Bill lit a cigarette and squinted. He spoke to Emma but gawked at Jennie. "Your sister is crazy, Em. I warned you not to let her come here. Once a loony always a loony."

"I'm not crazy," Jennie defended, narrowing her eyes. If she was a cat, she would have jumped on him and clawed his face.

"Bill!" Emma hushed him and took hold of Jennie's hand, like she was a child. "Honey, are you sure your friend said his name was Seth Thacker?"

"Of course, I'm sure." Jennie wriggled out of Emma's grasp, irritated.

"How old is your friend?"

"I don't really know. Five, maybe ten years older than me. I'm not sure." Jennie caught the look that flew between her sister and brother-in-law. "What's going on? Why are you two acting strange? Do you know Seth?"

Bill leaned against the porch railing and chuckled. "Oh, we know him, all right. Or I should say we've heard of him. He's a part of this town's history."

Jennie crossed her arms over her chest and pursed her lips. "Well, I should imagine so, if he's the lighthouse keeper."

Again, Emma and Bill traded glances.

"Honey," Emma said gently, "Seth Thacker *was* the keeper of the lighthouse, about fifty years ago. He died when he was in his early twenties."

Without skipping a beat, Jennie said, "Then this must be his son or grandson. Lots of people name their children after family."

"Not possible," Bill said. "Seth Thacker never had kids. He committed suicide a couple of nights before he was to marry the innkeeper's daughter."

"Suicide?"

"Bill!" Emma exclaimed again, clucking her tongue.

"Who was he to marry? Which innkeeper's daughter?" Jennie asked.

Emma sighed. "Poor Seth Thacker was engaged to the daughter of the man who established this inn, the Lake House. It was said that Seth would flash a secret message to Marie from the lighthouse every night at the same time. The story goes that she would sit in the window of her room and reply to his message by placing a lit lantern in the window. It was a symbol of her love and devotion."

Momentarily confused, Jennie frowned. "Then my Seth is a nephew or a cousin."

"Seth Thacker didn't have any family," Bill stated.

Her next comment bit. "Then it's a coincidence that two men have the same name."

"That would be a mighty odd coincidence," Emma replied. Her brows furrowed.

Jennie was afraid to ask the next question. "Which room was Marie's?"

"Yours," Bill blurted.

A few moments passed in silence. "Why did Seth"—she could barely say his name—"commit suicide? Does anyone know? Did he leave a note?"

Emma explained. "That night, Marie didn't light the lantern. The lighthouse keeper was so worried that something had happened to her that he rowed straight across the lake and burst into the inn. The lobby was deserted at the time, so he ignored all the rules of propriety and ran up the stairs to her room. When he burst through the door, he found her in the arms of another man." She stopped and looked to Bill to finish the story, and he appeared happy to oblige.

"According to legend, Seth always carried a revolver on him, in case of running into a gator. He shot Marie and the other man dead and then fled to the lighthouse, where he climbed the stairs to the observation deck and flung himself over the railing. The fall broke his neck." Bill took a long drag from his cigarette and ended with, "If you've been socializing with Seth Thacker, your friend is a ghost."

Jennie felt like she was slipping on ice, skidding down a mountain with nothing to break her fall.

Emma grabbed her hand again. "There has to be some explanation. Perhaps you misunderstood his name."

"I didn't misunderstand."

"Did he tell you definitively that he was the lighthouse keeper?"

"Yes." Her thoughts wandered back to that discussion. When she'd questioned Seth, he'd stared at her blankly before answering. Had he been lying? She suddenly felt very tired and confused. "I think I'll go to bed now." She stood and clutched her stomach, feeling like she was going to vomit.

"Wait," Emma said.

"No. I don't want to talk about this anymore. Good night." She passed by Bill, wanting to slap him when his mouth lifted in a smirk.

As she opened the front door and stepped into the lobby, she heard him say to Emma, "Your sister belongs back in the nuthouse, and by God, I'll see that she returns if she does anything to sully our reputation in this town."

As if he wasn't doing that all by himself, Jennie thought with bitterness, as she quickly strode up the stairs.

CHAPTER SEVEN

After crying herself to sleep, Jennie woke early the next morning and went downstairs in search of Emma. "I need to find him," she told her sister. "You were probably right last night. He must be sick or hurt."

"I'm going with you."

"You don't have—"

"I want to," Emma interjected. "Give me just a minute." She found someone to man the front desk and then held her skirts up and traversed the stairs two at a time. Jennie nervously shifted from one foot to another while waiting. "Bill will watch the kids," Emma said, upon her return.

"Did you have to bribe him with a bottle of whiskey?" Jennie knew she shouldn't have said it, but if her brother-in-law had his way, she'd be put on a train and sent back to the asylum before the end of the week.

"I hear the gossip about my husband," Emma said. "Deep down he's a good man. Or, at least, he used to be."

Jennie wished she could tell her sister that she was being made to look like a fool. Aside from being a drunkard, Bill had propositioned her and had most likely made plays for other women. Instead, she replied, "Forgive me for saying that, Emma. I'm on edge."

"I understand. Let's go and see if we can learn the whereabouts of your friend."

They found Mr. Butterfield and Butch at the post office, and he gave permission for them to use his boat.

Luckily, he hadn't been angry with Jennie when she returned yesterday after the storm. In fact, he'd only been concerned for her safety and had squeezed her into a bear hug when he saw she was all right.

"You've become dear to me," he told her.

"You're a good friend," Jennie responded, kissing his cheek.

"Take all the time you need," he said, helping both women into the rowboat.

"I can't believe you know how to row a boat," Emma exclaimed, after they were on the water. She gripped the sides with white knuckles, but relaxed once they were halfway across the lake.

"There are many things you don't know about me," Jennie said.

After the boat thudded onto land, she anchored it and then reached for Emma's hand and assisted her out. "Come on. Hopefully, he's in the keeper's cottage." They lifted their skirts and trudged through the sand. Jennie knocked on the door. When there was no answer, she peeked into the window. A gasp rose in her throat.

"What is it?" Emma asked. "Is he hurt?"

Jennie turned the knob to find the door unlocked. When she entered, her hand covered her mouth. The room was empty. There was no rocker, no footstool, and no kitchen table. Cobwebs clung to the corners of the room. Had those webs been there before? She couldn't recall. A thin layer of sand covered the floor, too, as if it hadn't been swept in weeks. Had love blinded her to these tiny details?

The hearth that had burned brightly after Seth started a fire while she stood shivering in wet clothes was now cold and dark. She flung open the kitchen pantry to find it empty. Then she ran into the bedroom and gazed at the empty corner where they had made love on a bed with creaky springs.

She felt like she'd walked into a nightmare. "I don't understand, Emma. He was living here! We cooked in this kitchen together. We spent hours talking in this room. While the storm was raging all around us two nights ago, Seth made a fire and we were cozy and warm. We slept—" Her words stopped mid-sentence and she felt the blood drain from her face.

Emma stared, her chest rising and falling in syncopated rhythm. Her mouth drew into a thin line.

Jennie could read her mind. "I love him!" she cried. "And he loves me." She placed her head in her hands, bewildered and afraid.

For what seemed an eternity, the sisters didn't speak. Finally, Emma said, "Let's go home. You need to rest."

From the tight expression on her face, Jennie knew her sister thought she'd lost her mind.

"I'm not insane, Emma. I met a man named Seth Thacker two weeks ago and we fell in love. He asked me if I wanted to live with him, here in this cottage." Suddenly, she remembered the drawing she'd done of him. "I have something to show you. It'll prove I'm not mad."

"I have something to show you, too," Emma said.

When they returned to the Lake House, Jennie excitedly showed Emma the sketch. "Do you recognize him? You must."

"No. I've never seen that face before. This town is small, Jennie. Everyone knows everyone. As Bill and I told you, there is no lighthouse keeper and there hasn't been for years." Jennie's shoulders slumped, and Emma's voice grew more tender. "We haven't talked about it, but it must have been a difficult time for you in the institution. You had to have been very lonely. Once you noticed the lighthouse across the lake, I'm sure it was quite an adventure to row yourself across and explore the island. It would be easy to lose yourself in imagination."

"What are you saying?"

"Is it possible that you've been so lonely that you dreamt up a friend?"

Jennie gritted her teeth. "I didn't dream up Seth." Her pointer finger stabbed at his likeness. "He's real. I'm not crazy."

Emma huffed and blew out an exasperated sigh. "Then this person you met was a stranger posing as the lighthouse keeper for some ridiculous reason. You're lucky he didn't murder you and chop you into little pieces." She placed her hand on Jennie's arm. "I'm sorry, but if there really was a man, he tricked you into believing he was someone he's not. He took advantage of your good nature and gentle spirit."

60

"He didn't," Jennie said, stubbornly. "Seth will show up. You'll see."

Emma looped her arm through Jennie's. "Come with me. I have something to show you now."

They walked several blocks and stepped through an iron gate. Ancient live oak trees dripping with Spanish moss towered over the town cemetery. It took some investigating, but when Emma pointed out the tombstone with Seth Thacker's name engraved in rock, Jennie's breath released in a jagged shudder. The inscription was heartbreaking and so impersonal.

> *Seth Elias Thacker*
> *Lighthouse Keeper*
> *Born 1835*
> *Died October 1859*

"This doesn't prove anything, except that this Seth Thacker died tragically," she said.

Emma's stance was firm. "It proves that *if* you really met a man at the lighthouse, he was a liar."

Jennie felt a chill creep up her arms like the brush of spider legs. If Emma was right, she'd been a fool. If her sister was wrong, she'd slept with a ghost.

****

For the next two weeks, Jennie made the trip across the lake every day in hopes that Seth would be there waiting. As she rowed, she pictured him standing on the shore when she arrived. He'd draw her into his arms, and his lips would move through her hair and over her neck. Lovingly, he'd explain that he had been called away suddenly that night and was sorry that he'd missed Becky's party. There had been no time to contact her, he'd say. An emergency had arisen. But he was back now and they would be together, now and forever.

Each time the rowboat made it to shore, disappointment sunk in. No Seth waited. The keeper's cottage remained cold and empty, as if no one had ever lived there.

As she rowed back to Tavadora, her shoulders shook with sobs.

At night, she stood by the window in her room and waited for the beam of light to appear and throb three times. But the lighthouse had also grown cold.

CHAPTER EIGHT

When another month went by without a word from Seth, Jennie began to lose hope that she would ever see him again. Since she'd believed he lived at the keeper's cottage when they met, and he never spoke of family, she had no idea how to contact him. The people she showed her drawing to in town claimed never to have seen him before. There was no address for which to write to him.

Surely, if he'd suffered an accident on the night of Becky's party, someone would have found him and she would have heard through the grapevine. If he'd been sick, he might have visited a doctor. In a last ditch effort, she questioned the only physician in Tavadora, but he'd not recalled treating a man matching Seth's description.

Jennie's heart was shattered, but she didn't dare show how much the loss meant to her. Emma was sympathetic and tried to help by keeping her busy around the inn. But Jennie had overheard Bill mention again that they should send her back to the nuthouse. His inappropriate behavior toward her was ammunition to use against him if it came to that, but would Emma believe a sister she barely knew over her husband of many years?

Going through the motions and forcing smiles she didn't feel became the norm.

About seven weeks after Seth had vanished from her life, she began throwing up in the mornings. At first, she assumed she'd contracted a bug from one of the children or a guest. But when Emma caught her vomiting into a bush one day while sweeping the veranda, her pale face said it all.

"Are you with child?" Emma asked point blank.

"I...I don't know."

"Well, I do." She grabbed Jennie by the arm and shepherded her into the hotel and up the stairs to her room, where she practically slammed the door behind them. "I guess you didn't sleep with a ghost after all! How could you do this to me after all I've done for you?" Her top teeth dug into the soft flesh of her bottom lip; she clearly struggled to maintain composure. "I can't believe you laid with a man you hardly knew. Now he's gone off and left you with a bastard!"

Jennie placed her palm on her stomach, reality sinking in.

Emma paced the floor, thinking. "You'll have to marry, and swiftly. There must a few bachelors in this town that will do."

"Marry a stranger?"

"You gave your body to one," Emma hissed. "What's the difference?"

"The difference is that I loved Seth and he loved me."

"Oh, right. That's why he took off without a forwarding address, is it?" She wrung her hands together. "What are the ladies in town going to think? It's bad enough that you've recently been released from a mental institution. Now you've gone and gotten yourself pregnant!"

"I don't care what anyone thinks." Jennie believed her sister should worry more about what the people of Tavadora said behind her back about her drunk, philandering husband, but she kept the spiteful remark to herself.

"Were you so desperate for attention that you let the first Tom, Dick or Harry that came along poke you?"

Jennie's gaze dropped to the floor. Her sister's words stung, but she wasn't going to sully the love she felt for Seth. "It wasn't like that, but if you want me to leave the Lake House, I understand."

Emma slid a shaky hand through her hair. "The best solution would be for you to marry anyone who will have you. I don't know where the money will come from, but somehow I'll scrounge up something to bribe whoever he is to keep his mouth shut about the paternity. When the baby comes, we'll say it's premature. No one in town will be the wiser." Emma smiled, proud of the plan she'd devised on the fly.

Jennie shook her head and gathered her courage. "I won't do it, Emma. I'll not marry a man I don't love, especially one who would take money to *have me*, as you put it."

Emma planted her hands on her ample hips. "Then what do you suggest?"

Sitting on the bed, Jennie had no idea. Seth was the father of her baby. He was the only man she wanted to marry. Apparently, he'd abandoned her, but she believed there was a good reason. Surely, he would not have if he'd known they'd made a child together that stormy night.

Inspiration came to her like the flood of tears that threatened to erupt. "I'll move into the keeper's cottage across the lake. That way, you won't be humiliated by my state as I grow bigger. I'm sure Mr. Butterfield will let me borrow his rowboat whenever I have need for it, and I'll find a midwife to attend to me when the time comes, if you don't want to help."

"There's nothing in the cottage. What will you do for furniture?" Emma inquired.

"I'll buy some hand-me-downs with the money I've saved from working here at the inn. I don't require much."

"What about food and supplies? I've paid you a pittance."

"I'll get by," Jennie assured. "I'll catch and eat fish from the lake every day if I have to." Although the idea of living alone on the island was frightening—as well as giving birth without the support of her sister— Jennie knew there was no other choice. She'd made her bed and now she had to lie in it.

"So be it." Emma left the room without a backward glance.

As Jennie rubbed tiny circles over her stomach with her fingers, the seed of her idea continued to bloom. Hopefully, Seth missed her as much as she missed him. Something was keeping him away right now, but he just might return to the lighthouse someday. If he did, she'd be waiting for him, and they'd be a family.

She smiled. Everything would work out all right. She simply needed to stay positive and have a little patience.

That belief fortified her as she packed her suitcase and glanced out the window to gaze upon the lighthouse that would soon be home.

CHAPTER NINE

September, 1928

Jennie was removing a tray of muffins from the oven while sixteen-year-old Laura filled another pan when a knock sounded on the door.

"Are you expecting friends?" Jennie asked her daughter.

"No, Mama. This afternoon a group of us are going on a picnic, but this morning is our time together. Yours and mine."

Jennie smiled. From the day she was born, Laura had been the sweetest girl, and she'd grown into a kind and considerate young woman. Not all girls would spend half their day baking with their mother. Laura was special. She had many friends, received high grades in school, and was almost a better sailor than her. Being raised by a mother alone had not hurt her.

Setting the tray on the cooling rack, Jennie wiped her hands on her apron. "I'm not expecting anyone either. It could be Blanche, but I was certain we made plans to play cards on Wednesday this week." Blanche was old Mr. Butterfield's goddaughter and had been Jennie's best friend for many years. She was also Laura's godmother, as she had been present for her birth, holding Jennie's hand, breathing alongside of her, and drying her tears when the contraction pains became too great to bear.

68

The early years on the island had been difficult with a small baby to care for and no steady income, but Jennie survived. Word eventually got around Tavadora that her cookies and bread were tastier than those sold at a higher price at the only bakery in town. With some word-of-mouth advertising by Blanche and Mr. Butterfield, she was lucky to garner some regular customers who didn't mind rowing their boats to the island to purchase her goods.

She was also able to earn a bit of income drawing portraits. Not only did she specialize in people, but she was commissioned to draw pictures of pets and homes, too. Sometimes even a favorite boat.

The third way she was able to provide for Laura and herself was due to Mr. Butterfield's generosity. He owned several fishing boats, and although the old rowboat Jennie had used was special to him, he no longer needed it. When he gifted it to her, completely refurbished, she took full advantage of the lessons he'd taught her and started her own company. Visitors coming to town were more than eager to pay good money for a boat tour around the lake and down the canal, where they were assured of viewing authentic wildlife, including turtles, gators, and beautiful shore birds.

Although it took a couple of years, Emma finally forgave Jennie her indiscretion and became a doting aunt to Laura—not to mention a loyal sister. Perhaps the reason she came around had something to do with Bill's mysterious death in the home of another woman, but

Jennie never questioned the good fortune that had brought them back together. Laura had grown up with cousins, family, and friends who loved her.

Jennie glanced around the small house that meant so much and held wonderful memories. Decorated simply, but with a feminine touch, there were colorful rugs on the floor, bright curtains at the windows, and paintings on the walls. She and Laura had been comfortable in the keeper's cottage all these years—comfortable and happy. All in all, it had been a good life.

A second knock came at the door. She opened it and was greeted by the crooked smile of a tall young man holding a leather briefcase.

"Good afternoon, ma'am," he said, tipping his cap.

She glanced around his shoulder to glimpse a small boat tied at the dock that Blanche's brother had built years ago. "Good afternoon."

He cleared his throat. "Are you Mrs. Sullivan? Mrs. Jennie Sullivan?"

"Miss," she clarified.

"Beg your pardon." His cheeks flushed. "I would like to introduce myself. My name is Linus Cavanaugh and I have come all the way from Orlando to meet you."

"Is that so?" Jennie turned her head to find Laura standing at her elbow. "This is my daughter, Laura."

"Pleased to meet you, miss," he said, politely.

Laura curtsied. "I'm pleased to meet you, too."

"Won't you have a seat in our garden, Mr. Cavanaugh?" Jennie asked. She gestured to the lighthouse, where years ago she had planted flowers on the other side of it and built two benches out of scrap wood. The spot was a place for meditation and inspiration. It was where she created many of her drawings. "It's your lucky day, as my daughter and I have been baking. You must be famished after that long journey, but it's much too hot inside to sit."

"I could do with a cup of water, if you don't mind."

"Certainly."

Laura showed him to one of the benches while Jennie retreated into the house and drew him a glass of water. She then took the last pan of muffins out of the oven and turned the oven off. "Muffin?" she offered, when she returned to the garden.

"Don't mind if I do." He heartily ate it and drank the water down in a long gulp. "Thank you, ma'am. The muffin was quite excellent."

She nodded her appreciation and noticed Laura smiling dreamily at him. Her daughter was at that age where girls began falling in love and speculating on the man they would marry.

Sitting beside Laura on the other bench, Jennie folded her hands in front of her. "Now, Mr. Cavanaugh, what can we do for you? Tell me why you've made the long trip from Orlando. Are you selling goods of some sort?" She eyed the case sitting at his feet.

71

"Goods? Oh, no, ma'am." He chuckled nervously. "I'm not selling anything. I came because...because I've brought news about someone you used to know."

"Really? Who would that be?"

"Benjamin Seawald."

Jennie stared. The name meant nothing to her, and she told him so.

"I believe you might have known him as Seth Thacker."

She felt her heart thunder in her ears. "Seth?" It had been so long since she'd spoken his name aloud. It felt odd upon her lips. She felt Laura's gaze, but didn't acknowledge it.

Linus picked the briefcase up from the ground and placed it across his lap. "Seth Thacker was not his real name, however. It was Benjamin Seawald."

"What?" She didn't understand. His name was not Seth but *Benjamin*? It took a second to wrap her head around the news. Who was this young man and how did he know her Seth? Or rather, Benjamin. Is that what Mr. Cavanaugh was telling her, that Seth's name was actually Benjamin Seawald? It didn't suit the man she'd loved, and still did love.

She'd dreamt of this day—well, not the day where a young man she didn't know brought news of her long-lost lover, but of the day when Seth entered her life again. After all the years longing and hoping, her wish had finally come true.

"Mama, who is Mr. Seawald?" Laura asked.

Ignoring her daughter's question, Jennie's hands began to tremble, so she stuck them under her thighs. "Did…did Seth, I mean Benjamin, send you?"

Linus shook his head. "Unfortunately, no. I'm very sorry to inform you that my father passed away three months ago."

"Your father?" It felt like Jennie had been punched in the stomach. "Dead?" Two blows at once.

He'd returned to her only to be taken away again. The world stopped spinning for a moment, sending her flying into a far-off land of memories—memories of the days they'd spent together, and that one magical night when unbeknownst to either of them, Laura had been conceived.

An involuntary cry, like the squeak of a mouse, escaped Jennie's throat. She felt a hand on her arm and heard Laura's anxious voice.

"Mama, are you all right? Do you need to lie down?"

Snapping back to the here and now, she gently shook her daughter off. "I'm fine, dear. The news is a shock. That's all. I knew Mr. Seawald a long time ago. I always thought we'd meet again." Somehow she managed to keep her voice from cracking.

"Was he a very good friend?" Laura asked.

Jennie and Linus exchanged knowing glances. "Darling, would you mind going inside and making a pitcher of lemonade? There are fresh lemons in the ice box. Add lots of sugar. I have a feeling Mr. Cavanaugh would like something stronger to drink than water."

Disappointment filled her face, but Laura did as requested. "Of course, Mama. Excuse me, Mr. Cavanaugh."

Once she was inside the cottage and out of earshot, Jennie lowered her voice and leaned toward Linus. "You said Benjamin was your father, but your name is Cavanaugh." It was still strange to speak of Seth as Benjamin.

"I should have been more specific. He was my stepfather, but he raised me from a young age. Although he was the only father I knew, my mother never allowed him to adopt me. She wished me to carry forward the Cavanaugh name."

"I see." Jennie stared at him trying to guess his age. Not one to beat around the bush, and having time to, since Laura could return at any moment, she asked, "When did he and your mother marry? What year was it?"

"They married on Christmas Eve, December twenty-fourth, nineteen-eleven. I was three years old."

Jennie's chest concaved. At least he hadn't been married when they made love, but it hadn't taken him long to move on from her either. The thought both saddened her and fired her blood.

Linus glanced at the cottage. "I suspect you don't want your daughter to hear what I need to tell you, so I shall speak quickly."

"I would appreciate that. Start with how you found me."

"After my father passed, my mother was so distraught she couldn't go through his personal items, so she asked me to do it. I finally got around to the task last week. Inside a chest in the back of his closet was a box of papers and documents. I went through them one by one determining which were of importance and needed to be kept and which could be thrown out." He cleared his throat. "I found one addressed to Jennie Sullivan at the Lake House in Tavadora, Florida."

"A letter? I never received any correspondence from him."

"If there were others, he didn't post them, but I suspect this was the only one."

He did think of me, Jennie thought. "Did you read the letter?" she inquired.

Linus looked her in the eye. "I'll admit I was curious, since I'd never heard your name mentioned in our household before. But I was raised to value privacy, so the answer is no. I did not read it. Instructions on the envelope said it wasn't to be opened until after his death. Not knowing when he'd written it, I almost threw it away, not wanting to hurt my mother if she somehow learned of it. Also, I didn't want to sully my father's impeccable reputation and the respect I held for him, in case you and he had become acquainted after he'd married Mother."

A shadow crossed his face, and Jennie understood he needed answers. She would not keep him in suspense nor hurt an innocent child, although he was now a grown man. "I met the man who raised you before he married. I loved him and I thought he loved me. But as it turns out, he left me for your mother." The last words came out harder than intended.

Linus bowed his head, and a sigh of relief escaped his lips. "I'm sorry. That must hurt badly. The man I knew was a fine man. He provided for my mother and me, and he treated me as his own son. I was proud to call him Father. Mother and I were lucky to have him as long as we did."

Jennie had thought him to be fine, too. But if he'd been such an upstanding man, why had he left without a word? Although she'd been a willing partner, the fact remained that he'd taken her virtue and vanished. Seth had left her pregnant to deal with the repercussions alone. She always suspected it had to do with learning that she'd spent time in an insane asylum. Now she knew. The truth involved another woman.

"How did you know he called himself Seth if you didn't read the letter?" she asked.

"Seth Thacker is the name printed on the return address on the envelope."

"Oh." She was quiet a moment. "How did he pass?"

"He had a weak heart."

Her head dropped to her lap. "I'm sorry for your loss."

"I'm sorry for yours, as well."

Her head jerked up to meet Linus's caring gaze.

The cottage door opened and Laura began walking toward them carrying a tray with glasses and a pitcher of lemonade.

Linus handed Jennie the letter and she hid it inside the pocket of her skirt. Her emotions ran deep. It would take time for her to process the news before telling Laura the truth. She'd grown up believing her father had died before she was born. In a sense, that *had* been the truth, but she was old enough now to hear the real story.

Linus stood and snapped the briefcase closed. "I must go now. I've kept you long enough."

"So soon? And before you try my lemonade?" Laura approached looking downhearted.

Obviously noticing her disappointment, he poured a glass and gulped it down. "Delicious! It's the best lemonade I've ever tasted. Thank you, Miss Sullivan, for going to the trouble."

She smiled. "You're welcome, Mr. Cavanaugh."

"Thank you, Mr. Cavanaugh, for coming all this way and personally giving me the news about my old friend." Jennie offered her hand to shake.

He shook it and nodded. "I only wish it could have been better news. Take care, both of you."

With that, he strode to the dock, and the two women watched him climb into his boat and depart.

"Shouldn't you be getting ready for the picnic?" Jennie asked Laura, as they walked back to the house.

"Yes, but first, tell me about your friend, Mr. Seawald. I never heard you mention him before."

Jennie patted the pocket holding the precious letter. She could hardly wait to read it. "When you return from the picnic, we'll talk. I promise."

CHAPTER TEN

After Laura left, Jennie sat in the rocker in front of the hearth and pulled the letter from her pocket and read.

My darling Jennie,

If you are reading this, it means I'm dead.

Please believe me when I say that I have loved you and missed you all these years. My heart has ached so badly that it has grown weak. As I write this, I haven't long in this world, but I could not depart it without letting you know how truly sorry I am for leaving you without so much as a word. The truth is I was selfish. I believed saying goodbye would hurt me too much, so I chose not to endure the pain. Little did I know that the pain would cling to me for the rest of my life.

I understand if you have never forgiven me for my cowardice, but I must try to explain what my situation was. I will do so in this letter in hopes that it somehow reaches your hands.

My name is Benjamin Seawald, not Seth Thacker, and I hail from Orlando. Gilbert Cavanaugh was my best friend and partner in a building company. One day there was an accident on the job. Several men were hurt, Gilbert among them. He was fatally injured. Because of safety issues that had not been properly dealt with, I held myself responsible for his death. The last words Gilbert spoke to me were to ask me to watch over his family. He left behind a wife, Pauline, and a young son, Linus. Out of a sense of duty—and guilt—I promised to marry Pauline and raise the boy as my own.

When I met you that day at the lighthouse, I had only just arrived in Tavadora the day before. Pauline believed I had business to attend to, but I'd really needed time to myself before the wedding—time to contemplate whether I was going to go through with it or not. I didn't love her, but I was torn. The boy, Linus, needed a father, and I did care very much for the child and his well-being.

Before I left Orlando, an acquaintance learned of my plans to spend a couple of weeks in Tavadora. When I explained that I needed somewhere private and quiet to stay, the man told me of an island and a lighthouse across the lake. He said the keeper's cottage had been abandoned but still had a few sticks of furniture inside, if I didn't mind a rustic ambiance. The house belonged to a family member, who was an ancestor of one of the last lighthouse keepers—a man by the name of Seth Thacker. After many years, whatever was left in the house was finally going to be removed. Until then, if I wanted to stay there, I was welcome.

Jennie took some steadying breaths and continued to read.

I hadn't intended on lying when you asked if I was the lighthouse keeper. It would have been too difficult to explain the truth, so in that moment, I said yes, having no idea that I'd fall in love with you. The lie seemed harmless enough, as did telling you I was Seth Thacker.

But as the days went by, you entranced me and I did fall in love—completely, madly in love.

I don't regret what happened between us the night of the storm. I've always hoped you didn't either. It was the most wonderful night of my life.

Please, dearest, forgive me. I did consider breaking my promise to Gilbert, but in the end, I could not leave young Linus without a father. I realized it the morning after the storm. A hasty retreat was called for before I could change my mind, because if I looked into your beautiful face one more time, I would have abandoned Pauline and the boy for you. So, I disappeared like a thief in the night.

Despite my feelings and the joy I experienced when we were together, my obligation was to my best friend. Pauline has been a pleasant enough companion and tolerant of the blue moods that have sometimes overtaken me. But the light that has truly warmed my heart through these years has been my son, Linus. It's been an absolute delight bringing him up, the child I never sired.

Jennie gasped at those last five words. If only he knew!

I pray you've led a happy life, Jennie. May God bless you and keep you.

> *Yours always,*
> *"Seth"*

She laid her face in her hands and wept. Her emotions had been constrained for so long. If only they could have built a life together. It was all she'd dreamed of and hoped for, especially after Laura was born. How she'd yearned for the day when Seth would return and meet his daughter.

If only she'd known where to find him. She would have written and asked him to come back—and he would have. She knew in her heart he would have, particularly if he'd known about Laura.

But Linus was correct. Benjamin had been an upstanding man. He'd sacrificed his own happiness to fulfill a promise and carry out a duty. She wouldn't have wanted a man who didn't make that choice. Besides, she suspected Benjamin's life had not been one of complete martyrdom. Linus was the proof in the pudding. He was a young man who had been raised with great care and an abundance of love.

Jennie wiped the tears from her eyes. She'd loved Seth, but she'd survived without him, just as she'd survived the year in the asylum, her brother-in-law's advances, and being gossiped about in the early years. In the end, she'd grown into a strong and capable woman who had raised a strong and capable daughter.

"Yes, Seth," she whispered, "my life is good."

****

When Laura returned later that evening, Jennie said, "Sit by me on the couch. I want to share something with you." She lay the portrait of Seth that she'd sketched almost seventeen years ago in her daughter's lap. It had been secreted away all these years.

"Is this him?" Laura asked. "Mr. Seawald?"

Jennie nodded. "I knew him as Seth Thacker."

Laura's head tilted, but instead of asking questions, she ran her finger over the picture. Jennie saw her daughter's chest rise and fall, and she expelled short puffs of air from between her lips. After several long moments of studying the picture, she said, "He's my father, isn't he?" Her voice came out barely audible.

Jennie placed her arm around her shoulder and nodded.

"I look like him."

"Yes, you do."

Laura laughed and tears sprang into her eyes. "I thought he was dead." She caught her mistake. "I mean, before now."

"I'm sorry I lied to you. I thought it would be easier for you than knowing the truth about us...about me, what I did." She meant sleeping with a man before marriage, but her stint in the asylum also flashed through her mind. That was another secret Jennie had kept from her daughter.

Laura looked at her strangely before it registered. "I don't care about the past, Mama. You must have loved him very much."

"I did. And he loved me." She extracted the letter from her pocket. "This is the proof. It's the reason

Mr. Cavanaugh came. If your father had known about you, he would have loved you, too."

Laura hugged her mother and clung to her a long time.

"I've always wanted you to be proud of me, of the life we've shared," Jennie said.

"I *am* proud of you, Mama. You've given me everything I ever needed. I wouldn't have wanted any other life."

They spent the next hour talking, laughing, and crying.

By bedtime, they were both emotionally drained. Although it had been years since Jennie tucked her daughter in, that night, Laura asked her to.

Jennie pulled the cover up to Laura's chin and kissed her forehead. "Good night, sweetheart."

"Good night, Mama." Before the light was doused, Laura demonstrated maturity beyond her years by ruminating on how one decision could completely change someone's life.

Life was full of decisions that could make or break a person, Jennie thought. All that mattered was how you chose to handle them.

She stepped outside and her gaze moved up the lighthouse. Ever since the night that Seth vanished, the light had remained dark. It was an unsolved mystery, as she never understood why or how it had shined for that short period of time.

She strolled to the shore and listened to the lapping water and the call of the night birds. A soft breeze stirred her hair, and the wind whispered her name. She closed her eyes and let the memories wash over her.

When Jennie opened her eyes, she stared across the lake to Tavadora and the hotel on the hill. Her breath hitched, and she placed her hand over her heart. There in the window of the corner room on the second floor, a lamp burned bright.

PART II

CASEY AND THE SEAPLANE PILOT

(The Present)

CHAPTER ONE

Summer, 2015
Tavadora, Florida

It was only three blocks from Casey Walden's bungalow to the Lakeview Inn, where she worked as General Manager, Controller, H.R. Director, and anything else her dad needed her to be. The historic property in her small tourist town was situated on Lake Tavadora and had originally been built in 1883 as a ten-room hotel called the Lake House. A woman named Emma Merrill had managed the inn for twelve years before being given the opportunity to purchase it in 1920. During her tenure, she oversaw the construction of two additional buildings across the road from the main inn, for an addition of 52 guest rooms. When she retired, the inn was handed down to her daughter Becky, and then to Becky's son, who changed the name.

The Lakeview had been Casey's father and mother's dream when they bought it five years ago as their retirement project from Emma Merrill's great grandchild. Now Mom was gone, and Dad had finally admitted six months ago that there were financial problems and he was unable to run the place on his own. Knowing he would lose everything if someone didn't do something, Casey stepped in.

A leisurely stroll through the historic district every morning at 7 a.m. helped clear her head and prepare for the myriad situations that occurred each day in the hospitality industry. Today, however, she was running late, so it was power walking all the way, which was difficult with a heavy tote bag slung over her shoulder and a mega-sized container of coffee in her hand.

Normally an early-to-bed girl because of her long and stressful days, she'd stayed up late last night to support André Frechette, her boyfriend of six months, in his business endeavors. He was a French Canadian who had come to town to make his mark as the finest chef in the area. Last evening, he had hosted a tasting for some of the most highly regarded food and wine critics in the greater Orlando area at his restaurant on the water, located a block from the inn. Their reviews would boost his already successful business.

Casey's feet pounded the cobblestone sidewalks in tempo with the throbbing of her head. Too much wine during the tasting had left her with a hangover this morning, something she hoped the 16 ounces of coffee would help alleviate. Today was not a good day to be distracted by a headache and queasy stomach. Payroll had to be done between a staff meeting and interviews for housekeeper and maintenance positions.

In her mind, she ticked off the numerous items needing attention. Deep in thought and not expecting traffic so early, she started across Third Street. The blast of a car horn stopped her in her tracks. Jolting, coffee splashed from the top of her container onto her dress. Stifling a scream, she nodded to the driver of the car and mouthed the words, "Sorry." After all, it had been her fault for not paying attention.

When the vehicle drove on by, Casey looked at the brown stain spreading across her yellow sundress and muttered, "Crap." At least she wasn't burned, but now she looked a mess. She could have turned around and run back home to change clothes, but her schedule was packed and there was no time to waste. She kept a sweater hanging in her office that she could wear to cover the stain.

As soon as she crossed the street, she tried her best not to glance at the shop on the corner, but it was no use. Every morning, despite her best efforts, she stopped to stare at the pink sign that read: *Candies by Casey*. The sign would be coming down any day now. Her gaze shifted to the door. A flyer taped to it said:

Petite Sweets
Opening Soon Under New Ownership!
Mini Treats That Will Satisfy Any Sweet Tooth

With a heavy sigh, she pressed her face to the big plate glass window. Inside, the light pink walls had been repainted high gloss white, a new tile floor had been installed over the original hardwoods that she'd sanded and refinished herself, and a sleek, ultra modern cabinet replaced the 1950s style candy case she'd worked so hard to find and then refurbish. The round wooden tables and cushiony chairs that once welcomed guests to sit and chat were gone.

"Don't keep doing this," she mumbled. "What's done is done. There's no going back." She started walking again, determined to take another route to work from now on.

As she passed the historic steam train sitting on the tracks and rounded the corner toward the inn, her gaze lifted. Beyond the property's grassy lawn, live oaks, sandy beach, and pier, Tavadora Lake sparkled like blue diamonds. As smooth as ice, the water melted into the bright sky, veiled in a magical silver mist. Squawking Herring Gulls wheeled through the air, and the slow-moving body of a small alligator glided along with gentle ripples trailing behind him. The breeze was as soft as a whisper. The view was picturesque and timeless, romantic and mystical.

Casey stood transfixed, memories flashing through her mind of so many good times she'd spent on the water. No matter how busy or stressed she became in her daily life, the lake could always calm her. Today was no exception.

From the beginning, much of life in Tavadora centered upon the lake. Excellent fishing provided bountiful dining—and still did to the local restaurants. Since the time of wagon travel, horse-drawn vehicles, steamboat transportation, and later the railroad, outdoor sports of boating, fishing, picnicking, and canoeing had always played an important role for visitors to the area. While some stayed for a short time, many came from colder regions to stay for the entire winter season, earning themselves the nickname of "snowbirds."

Not much had changed since 1880. Snowbirds still overran the town from October through April. But the locals didn't complain. Those folks brought in money and helped keep many businesses, like the Lakeview, afloat.

Inhaling a breath of fresh air, Casey caught the eye of Jack Butterfield, who stood on one of two piers that jutted out from the shore. His constant companion, Butch, a lively Jack Russell, sat at his feet. She waved and Jack waved back.

Legend was that he was the ancestor of one of the first settlers in town and had been a boat captain since anyone could remember. A fisherman in his younger days, he now gave excursions around the lake in his pontoon boat, the *Jennie,* which he moored on the north dock. He was fodder for local myth. Many joked that he was immortal, having spent his entire life on Tavadora Lake and never seeming to grow any older.

No one knew his true age, and he had no living relatives to spill his secrets, but it was generally assumed that he was way past sixty. Nevertheless, his back was straight as an arrow and his muscular biceps were envied by much younger men. Seemed he and Butch never ran out of energy. Today Jack wore his usual attire: loose trousers, a white short-sleeved shirt, and a captain's hat. Thick silver hair contrasted with his piercing blue eyes that mischievously glinted even from this distance. While more than happy to hand out advice to others, when asked about details of his own mysterious life, his lips were sealed.

Casey's gaze slowly shifted from Jack and Butch to the seaplane docked at the south pier. The white and blue plane was big enough to hold at least six people, she guessed. Since it wasn't unusual for guests to tie their boats and the occasional seaplane at the inn's dock, she thought nothing of it—even though it was far too early for guests to be checking in.

Shrugging her shoulders, she turned and cut across the old railroad tracks that ran parallel to the hotel. As she entered through the back of the house and passed by the laundry room, she glanced down at the stain on her dress. It had dried into a brown blob the shape of Texas.

"Morning, Miss Walden," Nan called, above the rumbling of the commercial dryers. She was folding towels on a large work table.

"Morning, Nan."

"Morning, Casey," a landscaper and server greeted in unison. One punched the time clock while the other waited his turn.

"Morning, Nick. Morning, Albert." She strode through the kitchen and said hello to the A.M. shift cooks, Mable and Eddie. "I'm sure you haven't seen my father yet, have you, Mable?" she asked the older woman who had been cooking at the hotel for over 30 years. She was putting the finishing touches on a plate of her delicious pancakes, which included three slices of bacon and a pile of crispy home fries.

"Yes, honey, I have. He's eating his oatmeal and fruit on the veranda." Her head snapped up and she hollered to Nick, who was fixing his black bow tie. "Take this plate out to Mr. Walden. It's for his guest. And hurry up about it."

"Yes, Miss Mable," Nick replied. He placed the plate on a tray and left the kitchen.

"My dad has a guest for breakfast?" Casey asked.

"He sure does, and the man looks like he can put the food away, so I fixed him extra. Good-looking fella. He's the new seaplane pilot Mr. Walden hired. Apparently, he flew in late last night. He's staying here at the inn, I was told."

"Seaplane pilot he hired?" Casey's mouth dropped open. Her dad had never mentioned anything about hiring a seaplane pilot. What on earth made him think they needed one? She struggled to keep her expression passive in front of Mable, but inside, her stomach suddenly churned. There was no budget for that kind of expense. The inn was barely breaking even as it was. If she hadn't taken control of the finances and management when she did, the place would have shut down, the employees would have lost their jobs, and Dad would have been on the street—or sleeping on the couch in her bungalow.

His impulsive nature was the reason he'd gotten into the mess he did, and why Casey had taken the reins six months ago. Despite her warnings and concerns when he and her mother had first told her they were buying the place, her stubborn father had thrown all of their retirement money into the rundown hotel, only to lose most of it due to poor management. And buying the Lakeview hadn't been his first bad decision. Although it was a heart attack that claimed her mother, Casey believed that a lifetime of dealing with stress over Dad's reckless behavior was what killed her.

Probably this seaplane pilot was one of his old war buddies or a long lost friend down on his luck. Joe Walden had always had a soft heart for misfits, but unfortunately, soft hearts could be smashed easily. More than one person had taken advantage of him through the years.

After quickly unlocking her office, Casey dropped her tote bag in a chair and placed the coffee container on her desk. Not remembering to slip into the sweater to hide the stain on her dress, she inhaled a deep breath and willed her racing heartbeat to subside. Even though she wouldn't show her anger in front of the pilot—who would be done before he even got started— her dad would get a piece of her mind the moment they were behind closed doors. No wonder he'd practically gone bankrupt. He had no idea how to run a business successfully.

She marched past the front desk and toward the front door leading to the veranda.

"Good morning!" Monica, the front desk attendant, called.

Casey glanced over her shoulder. "Morning, Monica."

"Mr. Walden is outside with the new seaplane pilot."

"So I heard."

"He's a real looker, too." There was a thrill in Monica's voice.

"Is that so?" Twenty-five-year-old Monica's idea of a handsome man was different from Casey's. Monica had been known to date a couple of guys who were much older than her, but if this man was anywhere close to Casey's dad's age, that was pushing it to the point of gross. "I'll be back in a minute. We have a few things to discuss about the upcoming weekend." She smiled, hoping she hid the exasperation she felt about her father.

She pushed the door open with her palm and looked to her right to find her dad sitting at one of the linen-covered tables. He smiled and chuckled at something his companion said. The man's back was to her, but she could immediately tell by the set of his shoulders, his shaggy blond hairstyle, and the T-shirt that stretched tight across his back that he was younger than she expected. No matter. He was history, whatever his sad story was. They simply couldn't afford an employee who wouldn't bring a direct, and a large amount, of revenue to the inn. She still needed to hire another maintenance man and housekeeper.

Casey cleared her throat and stepped toward the table, stopping behind the chair of the other man. "Good morning, Dad."

His eyes met hers, and his Adam's apple slid up and down in a gulp. With a glance at the man across from him, he scooted out from the table and stood. "Hi, honey. You're here early."

"I'm always here at this time, Dad." She wanted to add that she was surprised to see him up at this hour, as he usually didn't appear from his room upstairs until at least nine, but there was no need to be rude in front of a stranger.

"Won't you have a seat, honey?" he asked.

"No thanks. I have a million things to do. But when you have a moment, I'd like to speak to you in my office."

"Sure thing, sweetie."

Casey's gaze flitted over the man's hunched back. The fork in his right hand stabbed at the pancakes, and his hand slowly moved to his mouth. Apparently, he was more interested in eating than meeting the owner's daughter who ran the whole place—as well as his destiny. Thinking her dad would introduce them, but seeing that he stood frozen with eyes as wide as a deer's in headlights, she stepped around the table to introduce herself.

"Hello, I'm Casey Wal—" The words stuck in her throat when she met the man's soulful gaze.

He wiped his mouth with a napkin and stood. Twinkling green eyes stared at her—eyes that she'd looked into more than a million times. She felt the color drain from her face. Every muscle in her body tensed. Those eyes belonged to the man she'd planned on spending the rest of her life with. But the two of them hadn't spoken in a year and a half...

Stunned into silence, it felt like time stood still. When she finally snapped out of her surprised trance, she uttered, "Tad."

He let out the breath he'd obviously been holding, and his lips tipped in a crooked smile. "Hello, Casey. It sure is good to see you again."

CHAPTER TWO

She sucked air deep into her lungs to gain composure. "Tad, what on earth are you doing here?" The memory of their less than affable parting flooded her mind, so her words bit more than she intended.

"Well, your dad—"

Joe interjected. "Tad is our new seaplane captain, honey. We can offer rides over the lake to our guests, as well as to other tourists in town. It'll bring in some much-needed revenue."

She wanted to remind her father that he'd nearly run the inn into the ground due to impetuous decisions and poor money managing, but this wasn't the time or place to call him out. She offered a weak smile. "Dad, as the G.M., you need to speak to me before any new employees are hired or new programs are implemented." She turned her attention to her former boyfriend. "There's been a misunderstanding, Tad. We simply don't have the budget. I'm sorry we've wasted your time, but there's no job here."

"Hold on, Casey," her father interrupted, softly. "I'm still the owner of this hotel. I don't have to run every little thing past you. I want Tad, and he's going to stay. I promised him the position."

Balling her fists at her side, Casey gnawed on her lower lip. "Dad…" She stopped abruptly when Nick strolled through the front door and onto the porch to ask Tad and Joe if they needed anything else.

"Please tell your cook these pancakes are the best I've ever tasted," Tad said, rubbing his stomach.

"I will, sir."

"We're fine, Nick," Joe said. "Thanks."

"Yes, sir."

After Nick stepped back inside, Casey lowered her voice. "Dad, you may be the owner, but you brought me on to handle all aspects of the business, and I'm telling you, we can't afford this. I'm sure Tad will understand."

Her gaze fused with Tad's, and he flashed the grin that used to turn her stomach upside down and inside out. "Sure, I do, Casey. It's no problem. I didn't come here to cause any trouble between you and Joe."

She was irritated with her father, and memories of her breakup with the man she'd promised her life to bubbled to the surface like hot lava. He'd been in Alaska for two years. Why was he showing up now, out of the blue? Narrowing her eyes, she asked, "Just why *did* you come back to Tavadora? And when did you become a seaplane pilot?"

Joe placed his hand on Casey's arm. "Let's all go inside to your office and talk this through. There are too many eyes watching and ears listening out here."

Only one other couple was having breakfast on the veranda, but Casey noticed the man and woman cutting glances their way. "All right, but there's not much to talk about," she responded, turning on her heel. Joe and Tad followed as she opened the front door and marched across the hardwood floors, ignoring Monica's curious stare. Once she'd led the men into her office, she closed the door and didn't bother to offer them seats.

Joe spoke first. "Casey, Tad needs a fresh start. I thought we could help him out. Besides, I thought you'd be happy to see him."

"What do you mean by a fresh start?"

Tad cleared his throat. "Joe, I appreciate what you're trying to do, but maybe I should go. My showing up like this with no warning has got to be a shock for Casey." A sympathetic glimpse flew her way.

"No need to be concerned about my feelings," she said. "I'm a big girl and can handle anything that's thrown at me. I've proven that over and over in the past two years."

His guilty gaze shifted to the floor. With a sheepish look equally as guilty, Joe stared out the window behind her. Casey closed her eyes briefly. The two men she'd loved the most had both let her down, but she was strong and had survived all her losses— Tad, her mom, and her dream. Her eyes snapped open when her dad spoke again.

"Think I'll give you two some privacy to figure this situation out. Anyway, you have a lot of catching up to do."

Before she could protest, he was out the door. That left Tad standing there looking at her with the same puppy dog eyes that had once caused her to melt.

"I've missed you, Casey."

She shook her head. "Don't say that. If it were true, you would have contacted me sometime in the last year and a half. You stopped all communication after six months. Did the phone and email services all shut down in Alaska?" Suddenly, she felt the floodgates opening and tears pricked the back of her eyes, but she refused to cry.

"I don't expect you to forgive me. It's...complicated."

"Oh, really?" The blood in her veins began to boil, but she kept her voice low and even. The walls in the 132-year-old hotel were thin. "Let me tell you the definition of complicated. Complicated is having the man you love leave you for some crazy adventure in the Alaskan wilderness. It's seeing your mother die from stress and heartbreak. Complicated is having to sacrifice your own dreams to bail your father out of his misguided ones. Could I make it any clearer?"

The silence hung thick in the air between them for several heartbeats.

"I'm sorry, Casey. I had no idea you'd lost the shop."

"Of course you didn't. And to be clear, I didn't lose it. I sold it, because I had to take over management of this inn. If I hadn't, my father would have lost everything."

Tad heaved a deep sigh. "I'm so sorry about your mom. And I know what the candy store meant to you."

Yes, he had. But her dreams hadn't mattered to him. He'd left anyway, to chase his own castle in the sky. Not wanting his pity, she changed the subject and repeated what she'd already asked.

"What did my dad mean when he said you need a fresh start?"

Tad waved her off. "Nothing. Forget he said anything."

Her fists planted on her hips. "Where have you been? What have you been doing? Did the hunting and fishing expedition company work out? Have you been in Alaska all this time?" She was asking too many questions for someone who didn't care anymore, but her mouth had a mind of its own.

"My problems are not for you to worry about," he answered. "I never should have called your dad."

Her heart clenched. "You contacted my dad?"

The sound a horse makes blew through his lips.

She shook her head, unbelieving. "You reached out to Dad but not me. Wow." Now her feelings were really hurt.

Before he could reply, Casey glanced at the door upon hearing a loud and familiar voice outside in the lobby greeting Monica. When her office door opened and André popped his head through, Tad swung around.

"Sorry," André apologized, glancing at Tad and then studying Casey. "Monica didn't tell me you were with a guest."

"He's not a guest," she clarified. "In fact, he was just leaving." She arched an eyebrow and motioned

André in, relieved to have her conversation with Tad interrupted. Her limbs were shaking.

Tad's gaze moved from her to André and then back to her, where it stayed. A glimmer of understanding crossed his face. "She's right. I was just leaving. Thanks for your time, Casey. And please, don't be upset with your father. He was just trying to help." He offered his hand to shake.

Hesitating for several beats, she finally slid her palm into his. Electricity sparked between them, and much to her dismay, her heart thumped double-time inside her chest. When he smiled, she quickly slipped her hand out and backed up a step.

He excused himself. As he walked past André and through the door, he said, "Guess I'll be seeing you around town, Casey. Joe didn't get a chance to tell you, but I'm back to stay."

She caught the look on André's face. His dark brows furrowed like he'd eaten a sour pickle.

Tad stopped and turned. "Oh, and by the way, Case, do you mind me keeping my plane docked at your pier for a couple of days? I need a little time to rent a spot at the marina or figure out some other plan."

"Sure." Simply wanting him to go away, she was willing to agree to almost anything.

"Thanks." He winked and exited her office. She could hear him whistling as he passed the front desk.

André turned and stared at her. "He called you by your first name." His hands spread out in question. "I thought he was a guest. Who is that guy?"

"Please close the door." He did, and she stepped behind her desk and plopped into the chair and nodded for him to take a seat. "He is—was—an old friend." She cracked her knuckles, a terrible habit that flared when she was nervous.

André's dark and brooding eyes caught with hers. "Are you sure he's not more to you?"

"What are you suggesting?"

"We've been together for six months, Casey. I know you pretty well. You crack your knuckles when you're anxious."

"Shoot. Why do you have to be so observant?" She stuck her hands under her thighs and let her gaze drift over him. Physically, he was as different from Tad as the sun was to the moon. Stocky in stature, his hair was dark and cut in a military buzz. Scruffy whiskers covered his chin. "I should have told you about him before now, but I didn't see any reason to."

"But obviously, now there's a reason." He leaned forward.

"There really isn't, but I don't want you to get the wrong idea."

He rubbed his hands together in anticipation. "Then start talking. I'm all ears, babe."

****

There was not an atom of air left in Tad's lungs. In his 32 years, he'd been thrown by a horse, a motorcycle, and a motorboat, but nothing ever knocked the breath out of him the way Casey did. The moment he saw her again, something strong and hot had expanded his heart until he was sure his chest wouldn't hold it. But she'd rejected him, just as he'd expected. What a fool he'd been to have left her in the first place. If he'd stayed with her in Florida, he wouldn't have gotten into the mess he did in Alaska.

He strode down the walk past the swimming pool to the pier, where he found Joe waiting next to his plane.

"How'd it go? Did she reconsider?"

Tad shook his head. "Nope. Thanks for giving it your best shot, but your daughter made it pretty clear she doesn't want me *or* my plane on this property."

"Did you even try to convince her? I remember the two of you got into some pretty good arguments when you were together, but you could always win her over."

Tad thought back. Some of their best times had been spent debating all kinds of topics. Although the discussions sometimes got heated, they were all in good fun. In the end, they would always kiss and make up—another kind of heat he hadn't forgotten.

"I lost the right to challenge her a long time ago. Besides, I'm not one to beg for a job. I'll find work somewhere else, maybe over on the other side of the lake."

Joe wrinkled his nose in disgust. "You can't give up. I know you still love her. You wouldn't have come back if you didn't."

"I came back because you told me there was a job waiting here. You failed to mention that Casey is running the show and there's no budget."

Joe shoved his hands into his front pockets and shifted from one foot to the other. "My pride is gone, Tad. So is my dignity. I made a mess of things and had to ask my daughter to bail me out of a bad situation."

"We both know why."

Joe nodded. "I wanted you for a son-in-law because I knew you'd take care of my girl and never let her down, like I let her mother down."

"But I did let Casey down. I took off to Alaska when she needed me the most."

Joe shrugged. "You made a mistake. Now you're back and you can fix it. Casey has a forgiving heart."

Even with a heart as big as hers, she would never forgive me if she knew what happened up north.

"You shouldn't get your hopes up, Joe," he said. "It looks like Casey has moved on. Some guy with a French accent is in her office right now, and I got the impression they're more than pals."

Joe rolled his eyes. "That's André Frechette. He's the owner and executive chef of that French restaurant over there." He pointed past Jack Butterfield's boat to the building with green awnings. A wooden deck sat over the water.

"Is Casey dating him?"

Joe nodded. "For about six months now, but he's the complete opposite of you. He's arrogant and

106

demanding and a workaholic. I don't care for the guy and have no idea what she sees in him."

Maybe the complete opposite of me is just what she was looking for.

Tad didn't want to hear more about Casey's love life. His gaze met Jack's. The old man was staring him down with a smile on his face. "If you'll excuse me, Joe, I want to go over and say hello to an old friend."

"Sure, Tad. I have some things to do, anyway, but let's have dinner tonight. And don't feel any pressure to check out of your room at the inn. I asked Monica to book you for the week."

"What's Casey going to say about that?"

Joe grinned. "Let me handle her. I'll meet you in the lobby around six-thirty." With that, he sauntered up the sidewalk and disappeared around the corner.

Tad walked toward the old boat captain, who gripped his hand in a firm shake.

"Tad Singer, is it really you?" Jack flashed him a welcoming grin.

"Hi, Captain. Nice to see you again."

"Good to see you, too."

Tad bent and scratched the cheeks of the Jack Russell sitting at Jack's feet. "How are you doing, Butch?"

The dog barked and licked his hand.

Jack's chin lifted, and his inquisitive blue eyes focused on Tad's seaplane across the way. "I see you've changed careers since you left Tavadora."

Tad smiled. "I got my pilot's license soon after arriving in Alaska. That's the one thing that turned out right for me up there. Flying has become my one true passion."

At the soft splash of water, Tad's head snapped toward the lake. An alligator that had to be close to ten feet long glided toward the dock. It stopped about a foot away, and its hooded lids opened. As its glassy eyes locked onto Jack's, Tad's eyes widened, and he slowly backed up a few steps.

"Well, look at who has come for a visit," Jack said.

"I've seen that mammoth before," Tad replied, remembering a time when he was a boy and fishing in a hidden cove with his grandpa. "That thing swam past me and Grandpa in our boat. If he had bumped us, we might have fallen into the lake and been goners. Nobody believed me and Grandpa when we told people how big he was." Despite the hairs prickling his arms, it was impossible to look away from the prehistoric-looking creature.

"That fella doesn't mean any harm." Jack's gaze locked with the reptile's. "We've been friends a long time. He comes to see me every once in a while, but on the rare occasion, he seeks out the company of other humans." He turned to Tad and squinted. "He doesn't show himself to just anyone, but luck follows those who have seen him. You always were a lucky kid."

Tad's eyebrows knitted together. "I haven't been as lucky as everyone thinks," he sighed. The gator continued to swim slowly in front of the dock. He hoped it wouldn't spring onto the pier and gobble up Butch, who didn't seem at all fazed. "How old do you think that thing is, Jack?"

His eyebrow cocked. "Age has no significance for those who are truly tied to this lake."

Although it was probably 97 degrees, a shiver ran up the length of Tad's spine.

When he looked at the gator, its mouth opened and shut, as if it was speaking. Then its lids closed over its eyes like shutters, and the reptile sunk under the water. After slowly turning in a semi-circle, it paddled away.

Jack chuckled and slapped Tad on the shoulder. "Good to have you home again, son. Will you take me for a spin in your plane one of these days?"

He nodded, mesmerized as he watched the gator's long tail splash through the water.

"Terrific!" Jack sounded pleased. "Let me know when you and Casey want to go out for a ride on the *Jennie*." He motioned to the pontoon boat with the blue and white striped canopy. "I'll take you for a sunset cruise down the canal. It's very romantic. Your girl will like that."

Tad suddenly snapped out of his fog. "She's not my girl anymore."

Jack winked. "That might not always be the case. I'll wager you didn't expect to come home again either, did you? But here you are. Anything is possible on the lake."

Lake Tavadora (The Trilogy)

CHAPTER THREE

Casey smiled and asked the right questions during the interview, but she barely heard the answers the potential housekeeper gave. Her mind was elsewhere—specifically on Tad Singer. What a shock it was to come face-to-face with him after two years. He'd hardly changed in that time. Still handsome, fit and trim, and that smile… It was the same sexy smile, but his demeanor in general was different. There seemed to be something sad lurking behind the friendly face. It bothered her, because in the three years they'd been a couple, Tad had always been upbeat and positive, almost to the point of annoying at times.

Could the subtle change she noticed have anything to do with that *fresh start* her dad had mentioned?

"Thank you, Miss Walden. I appreciate your time."

The voice brought her back to the here and now. The young woman sitting across from her had her hand out ready to shake. Casey snapped out of her daydream.

"I like you, Sarah. If you want the job, it's yours."

Sarah grinned. "Really? Just like that?"

"Just like that. You can start tomorrow if you're able. Our executive housekeeper will train you."

"Yes, ma'am, I'm able and ready." She pumped Casey's hand. "I'll be here bright and early in the morning."

"Eight o'clock will be fine."

"Yes, ma'am. Eight o'clock it is. Thank you!"

"You're welcome. And you don't have to call me ma'am. It makes me feel old. I answer to Casey or Miss Walden, whichever you prefer. You'll see we're like a family around here."

Sarah stood up. "Yes, ma—, I mean…Casey."

When the young woman left her office, Monica strode in. "Did you hire her?" she asked.

"Yes, I did. And I also hired the second man who interviewed for the maintenance position." She closed the file that lay on her desk. "We're at full staff now. I hope everyone stays put for a while. We finally have a good group, and we're running like a well-oiled machine."

"Thanks to you," Monica complimented.

Casey shrugged. "It takes commitment from every member of the team."

"Is that cute blond guy with the seaplane going to be a member of the team?" Monica was practically drooling. But who could blame her? Tad was very attractive.

"No, he's not. We can't afford him."

Monica frowned. "How much was he asking?"

Casey realized they hadn't even gotten that far. She had no idea what her father had promised Tad for a salary, but whatever it was, they couldn't afford it. "I didn't give him the opportunity to discuss wages," she admitted. "We don't need to offer seaplane rides. Guests and tourists can go across the lake to the Flagler brothers if they want to fly over the lake."

"That's exactly why we need our own pilot," Monica stressed. "If you hire—what's his name anyway?"

"Tad Singer."

"If you hire Tad, ladies will flock here just to stare into that good-looking face and spend a half an hour with him. Plus, you'll take a piece of the pie away from the Flagler brothers, of course." Her lips curled in a snarl. "I dated one of those brothers for a while and he cheated on me. I'd love to see their business sink." She became excited. "Maybe you should talk to Tad again. You never know, he might be well off and flies planes for fun and doesn't need much money."

Casey chuckled. "Believe me, he's not rich."

Monica was observant and had good intuition. Her eyes enlarged. "You *know* Tad, don't you? Who is he, an old boyfriend or something? I did notice your dad seemed pretty chummy with him."

Certain that her flaming cheeks gave her away, Casey confessed the truth. "If you must know, Tad and I dated for three years."

"Wow! You lucky dog!"

"Shhh," Casey admonished gently. "Keep your voice down, will you?"

"That's a long time. What happened?"

"He went to Alaska two years ago to start a company with some long-lost childhood friend.

Apparently, he's been taking wealthy people on hunting and fishing expeditions in the wilderness."

The lines between Monica's brows pinched. "And you didn't go with him?"

"I couldn't. I'd just signed the lease on my candy shop. Plans were in place, equipment was purchased, inventory was bought, and I was about to make my dream come true. After eleven years of working my butt off at two jobs and saving every penny I earned, Candies by Casey had finally become a reality. There was no way I was giving that up. Tad was too selfish to stay here and support my dream. He chose to run off to the northern wilderness for a risky adventure and go into business with a guy he barely knew."

She hadn't intended on saying so much, but it was too late to reel the words back in. It was also too late to stop the knot from twisting in her stomach. It had been a long time since she'd talked about Tad. His departure and absence had hurt like hell, but she thought she'd buried the feelings—until now. It was a good thing she was sitting, because her heart suddenly gave a lurching thud that threatened to buckle her knees.

"I'm sorry," Monica said. "That *was* pretty jerky of him."

Casey agreed, but she'd already trashed him enough, without really intending to.

"And then you had to give up your candy shop to run this place. Gosh, that sucks."

Yes, it did, but there was no going back. Casey plastered a smile on her face. "Life goes on. I'm over it. And him."

Thankfully, the phone at the front desk rang just then, and Monica bolted to grab it.

Casey leaned back in her chair and sighed. "I *am* over him. I really am."

****

It was 6:15 when she finally closed and locked her office door. She had told André that she'd meet him at the restaurant at 6:45. Although he'd already held a big shindig last night, his investors were in town tonight and he wanted her to meet them and join them for dinner. It had been an emotional and tiring day, but she'd promised. If she hurried, she'd have just enough time to get home, take a shower, change clothes, and make it to *Chez André* on time.

Just after she wished a good evening to Mary Beth, the P.M. front desk agent, she turned and nearly smashed into Tad. The encounter startled her so much, the tote bag on her shoulder slipped off, and the financial report she planned on reading after dinner fell from her hands. In her haste to get the large report copied, she hadn't stapled the pages. Now, they lay scattered all over the floor.

"Crap," she muttered. "I don't have time for this."

"I'm so sorry," Tad said. "It was my fault for surprising you." He bent to begin picking up the sheets of paper.

She bent at the same time, and the two of them bumped heads.

"Ow!" She winced and rubbed her forehead.

"Are you okay?" he asked, reaching for her arm.

She jerked away, afraid of her reaction to his touch. "I'm fine." When she dropped to her knees and started gathering the papers, she said, "Why did you sneak up on me like that?"

He squatted and did the crab walk around the floor, making quick work of plucking the loose papers into his fingers. "I just wanted to say hello. I didn't mean to scare you. Honest."

Once all the sheets were in her hands, albeit in a jumbled mess, Tad lifted her tote from the floor and opened it. She began stuffing the papers inside. "I'm really sorry, Casey. Is your head all right?"

It was throbbing with the beginnings of a headache. "I'll survive." She checked her watch and realized she had less than half an hour to get home and back.

The scent of Tad's familiar cologne suddenly caused her nose to twitch. Her gaze moved over him, from the top of his surfer-blond head to the leather penny loafers on his feet. Seeing him in jeans that molded perfectly to his body and a baby blue button-down shirt stirred a stew of unwanted memories. He always did clean up good. "Are you going somewhere

115

tonight?" she asked, immediately regretting the personal inquiry.

He smiled. "I'm meeting your dad here in the lobby and we're having dinner together. Would you like to join us?" His voice was like caramel, soft and delicious. Living up north hadn't erased his sexy southern drawl.

"No thanks. I have a date tonight."

"Oh." His smile faded, but only briefly. "With the cook I met today?"

Taken aback, a wisp of a smile played upon her lips. "André Frechette is not a cook. He's the executive chef and owner of a lovely French restaurant. Maybe you saw it when you flew in. *Chez André* is located a block up, next to Jack's boat dock. It sits right on the water."

"I saw it," Tad said, grinning. "The guy doesn't have much of an ego, does he?"

Her eyes narrowed. "What do you mean?"

"He must be pretty self-absorbed to name his restaurant after himself."

Casey *had* thought it a little strange when André proposed the name, but Tad pointing it out got under her skin. "André is a confident man," she defended. The memory of Tad telling her he was leaving with or without her flashed through her mind like a lightning storm, sparking her temper. "There's a big difference between confident and self-absorbed, which you know a thing or two about." Her sharp words seemed to slice through him, and she immediately regretted them. "I'm sorry, Tad. I shouldn't have said that."

He chewed on his lower lip. "You have nothing to apologize for. You're absolutely right. I deserved that and more." A distinct hum mushroomed from him, and she felt the vibration between them like a tuning fork.

"Maybe another time," he said.

"Another time for what?"

"To go out together. I'd love to take you to dinner some night and grab a cupcake afterwards, or we could motor a boat to the island and sit by the lighthouse and point out the constellations in the sky. You used to enjoy simple dates like that."

Did he think reminding her of good times would change anything? She'd spent the past eighteen months building a bulwark against the black spaces that came with his leaving. With her heart beating faster, she reached for calm. "We're not going on a date, Tad. There's no point in us seeing each other anymore than is necessary, is there?"

His lips curved sideways. "I'd like to think there's still something between us."

Silence danced around them while she tried to decipher his comment. Suddenly realizing Mary Beth was eavesdropping, which she couldn't help since they were standing in front of her, Casey said, "I have a boyfriend, Tad. And I really have to go. Please excuse me." She strode toward the dining room only to realize he was following.

"Good night, Case."

"Good night," she said, over her shoulder.

"It's really great to see you again. You look wonderful, by the way."

"Thank you." If she returned the compliment, he would certainly get the wrong impression. Instead, she tossed a hand in the air and kept walking.

Before she reached the door to the kitchen, he said, "Thanks for letting me stay here at the inn this week. I really appreciate it."

Casey halted and turned around slowly.

"Uh-oh," he said, grinning sheepishly. "Don't tell me. Joe forgot to mention that he'd booked me a room."

"That's right. It seems my father has become quite forgetful lately. I suppose he comped it, too."

Tad shrugged. "If it's a problem and you need me to get out, just let me know. I can sleep in my plane."

"Your plane?" This was mind-boggling. Did he expect her to believe he didn't have enough money for a hotel, or no friends he could bunk with? He'd only been gone two years. He still knew plenty of people around town. She glanced at her watch again and shook her head. "I don't have time to deal with this right now. You can stay until Friday, but no longer. We have a full house checking in that afternoon. Check out's at eleven."

"Thanks, Case. You're very generous, considering."

"Whatever." Too much time had been wasted already. Now she'd have to forego a shower, but if she rushed, she might be only five or ten minutes late in getting to *Chez André*.

As she strode through the kitchen door, she heard Tad say, "By the way, my room is very comfortable, especially the bed."

A flame sizzled through her at the image his suggestive comment invoked, but she refused to turn around or acknowledge it in any way. Tad was her past. André was her future. And she mustn't keep him waiting.

CHAPTER FOUR

"No way, Joe. I'm not going in there." Tad froze in his spot in front of the door to *Chez André*.

Joe chuckled and gave him a slight shove. "Ah, come on. I don't like the guy, but he cooks well. He makes a killer cassoulet, and I could eat his cream puffs all night long. I'd pay ten bucks for the homemade French bread alone."

Tad shook his head. "When did you become such a connoisseur of French food?"

"Since my daughter started dating the owner and insisting I expand my culinary horizon."

"Let's go somewhere else. I don't like fancy food, and I don't want to be anywhere near Casey's new boyfriend. You must be out of your mind bringing me here. I thought you liked me."

Pushing the door open, Joe said, "I do. You're the son I never had."

Tad smiled. "You stepped in when my own dad left Mom and me. Then when she died, you and Casey were both there for me as family. And then..."

Joe slapped him on the back and interrupted his reverie. "Trust me about this place. There's a method to my madness."

Shrugging, Tad followed him inside, and they were led to the deck and a table with a large striped umbrella. "Would you gentlemen care for a glass of wine?" the server asked.

"Sure, I'll have a glass of red," Joe said.

"Sweet tea for me," said Tad.

"Coming right up." The server handed them menus and went over the evening specials. "I'll be right back with your drinks."

Tad began to scan the menu. Apparently knowing what he wanted to order, Joe didn't bother to open his. His eyebrow arched in curiosity. "No wine, Tad? Not even a beer?"

He pulled in a breath. "I gave up alcohol in Alaska. It always made me sick anyway."

When the server returned and asked if they were ready to order, he settled on ratatouille. It was one of the few things on the menu he recognized. When they were left alone again, he said, "Why did you really bring me here, Joe? I don't think it's just for the cream puffs."

He glanced toward the door and smiled. "Perfect timing."

When Tad's gaze followed, his chest tightened upon seeing Casey being escorted onto the deck by the hostess. Her curly chestnut hair was piled on top of her head, and she was an absolute knockout in a form-fitting black sleeveless dress. Topping off the stunning look was a string of pearls around her neck, high-heeled sandals, and a small clutch in her hand. He couldn't help but let his gaze drift from her shapely legs, past her small waist, and to her cleavage gently spilling from the top of the dress. When his eyes moved to her face, he jolted. Casey's brown eyes were locked on him, and her nostrils flared with rage.

"Chef said to seat you at the corner table," the hostess said to Casey, as they neared.

"Thank you, Beth," she replied. "I see that my father is here tonight. I'll say hello and then seat myself."

"Yes, Miss Walden. I'll let Chef know you're here."

Casey stopped at their table.

"Evening, honey," Joe said.

Good evening, Dad." Her icy gaze swung between the men, causing Tad to flinch. "What are you two doing here?" Although the words hissed through her teeth, what appeared to be a forced smile was glued to her face.

"We came to enjoy a nice French dinner," he replied. "No law against that, is there?"

Her eyes fluttered closed briefly and reopened. It was obvious she struggled to keep her cool. Her voice was low and measured. "No, Dad, it's a free country and you can eat wherever you please. But you knew I was coming here to meet André's investors this evening. If I didn't know better, I'd think you deliberately planned to bring Tad here tonight to sabotage the meeting in some way."

Joe feigned hurt. "Honest, honey. I had a craving for cassoulet, and I wanted to catch up with Tad. I totally forgot you'd be here tonight."

When she leaned over to talk even more quietly, Tad caught a whiff of her perfume and felt his head grow light. She always did smell like a flower garden.

122

Her eyes flashed. "I thought you two had already caught up. After all, you've both gone out of your way to make me look like a fool by communicating behind my back." She looked at Tad. "You don't contact me for a year and a half, but you reach out to my dad when you need help? What's that about?" Her gaze then shifted to Joe. "And you promised him a non-existent job that we can't afford. Now you're both trying to wreck an important evening for André."

Seeing the pain in her eyes, Tad knew it was time to speak up. "I don't know Joe's motives, but I'm not here to ruin anything, Casey. I'm really sorry for the trouble I've caused already." He stood. "If it'll make you feel more comfortable, I'll leave the restaurant, and I'll also leave the hotel and move my plane. The last thing I ever intended by coming back to Tavadora was to hurt you more than I have."

"Very noble of you, Mr. Singer."

Having been too immersed in the conversation with Casey, Tad hadn't seen the man approach. Neither had she, because Casey jumped when the Frenchie touched her shoulder.

"André, I didn't hear you behind me."

"Sorry to frighten you, sweetheart." He cut a sly glance at Tad and held out his hand to shake. "We met earlier today but weren't officially introduced. Casey told me your name. I'm André Frechette, owner of this fine establishment."

There was no reason to humiliate Casey further, so Tad acted a gentleman and shook the guy's hand.

"Good evening, Joe," Frechette said.

Joe nodded.

Frechette placed his arm around Casey's waist and squeezed her to his side. "If you don't mind, gentlemen, I need to steal my girl away. I'm showing her off to some very important people, and they've just arrived." He acknowledged the three suits at the corner table who were being seated by the hostess.

Although he'd just promised not to make a scene, Tad couldn't help but speak his mind. "Casey is a beautiful woman, but there's so much more to her than being someone's arm candy," he said, unsmiling. "I hope you know that."

"André does know it," she said, blushing slightly.

Frechette grinned, but it seemed disingenuous. Tad waited for him to address his comment but got no response. Instead, he said to Casey, "We mustn't keep our guests waiting, love." As an afterthought, he told Tad and Joe to "Enjoy your dinners."

As he tugged Casey toward the corner table, she glanced over her shoulder and locked eyes with Tad. This time the fire was gone, replaced by surprised confusion.

Wishing he could whisk her into his arms and haul her out of there, his heart thrashed inside his chest.

"That was a good dig," Joe chuckled. "I know you still love my daughter. I saw it in your eyes this morning, and I see the emotion in them now. That's why I brought you here tonight, so that you could confirm what I already knew—that you and Casey are meant to be together."

"She doesn't want me anymore, Joe."

"Phooey. I saw a spark in her eyes, too."

"That was pure unadulterated anger."

Joe slapped the table with his palm. "She might not think she wants you right now, but deep inside, she still loves you, too."

Tad wished he could believe that. He glanced across the room again to see her smiling and shaking hands with the three suits. Frechette ran his hand down her back and let it rest on her hip. Tad gritted his teeth. "I can't stand to see her with that guy."

Joe laughed out loud. "That's the Tad I remember. I've done my part bringing you home to Tavadora. Now it's up to you to win her back."

Just then the server delivered their meals. Joe took up his fork and licked his lips. "Sit down, son. Despite how we feel about the chef, he does know his way around a kitchen."

Tad glanced one more time across the deck to see Frechette place a kiss on Casey's cheek. Then he pulled his wallet from his back pocket and slipped a twenty dollar bill from it and laid it on the table. "This should cover my part. You can have my dinner, too, if you want it, Joe. I've lost my appetite."

Without another look back, Tad left the restaurant.

CHAPTER FIVE

Despite being exhausted from a second night of eating and drinking, Casey needed to stop off at the inn before heading home. She'd forgotten to tell Mary Ann something important that had to be relayed to the night auditor.

The moment she walked through the front door, she heard laughter and turned her head. Sitting in the hotel bar was Tad...and Monica. The sight of them together shouldn't have bothered her, because she'd gotten over him a long time ago, but it did. Although she liked Monica, her personal life was an open book. She'd admitted to being attracted to Tad. It was no wonder she'd apparently sought him out and was now shamelessly flirting with him.

As if an invisible string was tied to his head pulling him like a puppet, his neck swiveled, and his and Casey's eyes latched. His smile disappeared and he pushed back from the counter.

"Don't go," Monica said, grabbing his arm. Her loud and slurred words were a sure sign that she'd had enough to drink.

When Casey saw Tad striding her way, she huffed and made a beeline to the front desk. She had just given Mary Ann a quick message for the night auditor when he sidled next to her.

"Hi, Casey. I didn't expect to see you here so late."

Not wanting to talk to him, especially in front of Mary Ann again, she stepped around the corner and headed for the back door. He followed her outside and down the ramp to the parking lot. When she stopped abruptly, he bumped into her.

She spun. "What do you want, Tad? I'm tired and I'm ready to go home."

He shoved his hands into his jeans pockets. "Let me walk you. It's late. You never know who might be on the streets."

Rolling her eyes, she said, "This is Tavadora, remember? The town practically shuts down at six o'clock. I'm capable of getting myself home in one piece."

"I'm sure you are. You were always independent and not afraid of anything. Those were two of the qualities I loved most about you."

Her heart started to beat fast in her chest, and she blurted a response without thinking. "When you left me to go to Alaska, I was very afraid."

His hands planted on her arms, and he stared directly into her eyes. "I'm so sorry for hurting you, Casey. You have no idea how I've beat myself up over that stupid decision. I was a fool, in more ways than one. I hope, someday, you'll be able to forgive me."

Shaking her head, she resolved to stay strong and not be affected by sweet talk. But dang it, being so near him aroused old feelings, and her body burned under his touch. Why did he have to look so good under the light of the moon?

"Please let me walk you home." His lips lifted in a lopsided smile.

"Are you drunk?"

"No, ma'am. I'm as sober as a nun in a whorehouse."

She almost laughed. He always did have a good sense of humor.

He crossed his heart with his fingers. "Sweet tea is the strongest drink I've had in over a year. I swear it."

"Do you also swear you weren't hitting on my front desk agent?"

"Who are you talking about, the brunette that was sitting next to me at the bar?"

"Yes. Her name is Monica and she works for me."

He made an X across his chest again. "She hit on me, but I swear I didn't lead her on. I was about to head for my room when you walked in. And I was going alone," he emphasized. "The only woman I'm interested in is you. It's always been you. I'm hoping you'll give us another chance."

The nerve! "How can you say that after all this time?" She extracted herself from his hold. "I accept you didn't mean to hurt me, but you did, and the hurt ran deep. Seeing you again has stirred up painful memories. There can never be us again, Tad. We're over and done with."

"Don't say that. Let me try to make it up to you. You're the real reason I'm here. Not the job."

She spoke politely. "I've moved on. I'm with André now. He cares about me."

Tad's arms folded across his chest. "If he cares so much, why didn't he drive you home tonight? If you were still my girl, there's no way I'd let you wander the streets on your own at this hour."

The breath caught in her throat. Although she didn't want to admit it, his comment struck a nerve. The fact was, she'd asked André to take her home, but he'd been too busy cleaning up and closing down the restaurant, even though he had employees who could do that. There was no way she'd let Tad know, however, so she sidestepped his remark. "First of all, I'm not wandering the streets. And secondly, as we just established, I'm not your girl anymore, so you don't have to concern yourself. Good night, Tad."

As she turned to walk away, he grasped her arm and swung her around. Before she could react, his mouth covered hers. His arms encircled her, drawing her tight to his chest, so close she could feel his heart beating. The heat of the kiss caused a flame to ignite deep inside. Spinning…spinning…her emotions ebbed and fell like the tide, and there was nothing to anchor her.

Breathlessly, Casey broke the kiss and stepped back. She would not allow herself to be manipulated, simply because they had a past. He'd been in the wrong. He'd been the one to ruin their relationship. Three years of her life had been wasted on him and his promises.

"Tell me you didn't feel that same old spark just now," he whispered.

She gritted her teeth. "The spark I felt for you flickered out long ago, Tad. All that remains of our relationship is a cold pile of ash."

He flinched, as though he'd been slapped, and the light in his eyes faded.

"You can stay at the hotel until Friday, and then you need to leave." With that, she strode through the parking lot and away from him as fast as her feet would carry her.

****

Pounding on the front door startled Casey awake. Through unfocused eyes, she could barely read the time on the digital clock sitting on top of the dresser. Was it really three a.m.?

Another loud rap had her bolting upright and slamming open the bedside table drawer. She reached for her revolver and slipped off the bed and stuck her arms through the sleeves of her robe. With her fingers clasped around the grip, and the gun held at her side, she tiptoed through the living room to the door.

When a third knock sounded and a familiar voice called her name, she peeked through the peep hole. What on earth was André doing on her doorstep at this time of the morning? She placed the revolver on the coffee table before unlocking the door.

"What's wrong? Has something happened?" She quickly ushered him into the house. "Is it my dad?"

"No, love. Your dad's fine, as far as I know." He kissed her lips and then made himself at home by sprawling on the couch.

Confused, she sat beside him and pulled the belt of her robe tight. "Then why are you here?"

"I missed you." His gaze shifted from her face to her body, and he flashed a wolfish grin. The robe was silk and clingy and wasn't all that sexy, in her opinion, but the look in his eyes said otherwise, expressing his intentions.

André scooted close and cupped his hand behind her head and pulled her toward him for another kiss. When he stood up and grabbed her hand and began to tug her in the direction of the bedroom, she dug her heels in and stopped him in his tracks.

"Where do you think you're going?"

"To bed, but sleep is the last thing on my mind." He pinched her bottom.

Not expecting the pinch, she yelped and slapped his hand. "Are you kidding me?" Her ire rose like a teakettle set to boil. "I have to get up in three hours, and I have a full day of work ahead of me." When he tried to kiss her again, she turned her cheek. "I mean it, André. Is that the only reason you came over here?"

Frowning, he said, "You've never complained before."

"You've never been quite this inconsiderate before."

131

"In what way am I being inconsiderate?"

She huffed, "If you don't know, maybe you should go home and think about it. Let me know tomorrow if you figure it out." She turned and marched to the door, signaling him to leave.

His dark eyes narrowed. "This is about that guy, Tad, isn't it? Your old boyfriend."

"What?" An irritated chuckle burst from her mouth. "This is about *you* thinking it's okay to wake me up in the middle of the night and have your way with me. Well, it's not happening. Good night, André." She held the door open and felt warm, humid air sift inside. When he didn't move, she nodded her head. "I'll talk to you tomorrow. I mean, later today."

"Is he coming over here tonight?" he asked with suspicion. "Is that why you don't want me to sleep over?"

His question was too ridiculous to answer seriously. "Technically, this is morning, and no, he's not coming over."

"Did you go to bed with him already?"

Now she was really peeved. Casey felt her cheeks heat with anger. "I'm not even going to dignify that with a response. Go home."

He crossed his arms over his chest and planted his feet apart to pose in a defiant stance. "Not until you tell me the truth. I saw the way you two looked at each other at the restaurant. Do you still have feelings for him?"

"Of course not!" Practically shouting, she closed the door so as not to alarm her elderly neighbor who had insomnia and tended to sit on her screened-in porch sometimes at odd hours of the morning and night. "I haven't even talked to the man in a year and a half. Tad Singer means nothing to me anymore."

André's face relaxed, and he rubbed his hand down her arm. "Then why can't I stay?"

She inhaled through her nostrils and let the breath rush from between her lips. Her words were so tart they could have spiced a pie. "Because, frankly, I'm annoyed with you. I've spent the past two nights supporting you at the restaurant, dressing up and playing nice for the food critics and your investors, and what do I get in return? You didn't even drive me home! And then you come here and pound on my door, scaring me to death, and wake me up from a deep sleep—which I needed very much, by the way—and expect me to jump at the chance to have sex with you. If I weren't such a nice person, I'd call you a really bad name right now."

"Hold on a minute."

She flung open the door again, unwilling to discuss the matter. "I'm exhausted. Please leave."

Hesitating briefly, he walked through the door and mumbled, "Whatever. Good night."

After she'd locked up and returned the revolver to the bedside drawer, she climbed into bed but was unable to go back to sleep. Her mind swam. It was

133

impossible to stop thinking about Tad, André, and the past eighteen hours.

Had she been too rough on André? *No*, the voice in her head confirmed. Since they'd become serious, she'd bent over backwards to support him in his dream, without much return to show for her efforts. Behaving like a horse's butt was inexcusable. *He didn't even apologize*, the voice reminded.

Then there was Tad. Did he think he could just waltz back into her life after all this time and things would go back to the way they were? Surely, he wasn't that naïve.

She smashed her fist into her pillow and curled her knees up to her chest. When she closed her eyes, it was Tad's face she saw swimming behind her eyelids. She touched her lips, still tasting his kiss, and her stomach fluttered. Her eyes popped open, and she flipped onto her back and stared up at the ceiling. "Why did you really come back?" she asked aloud.

The only woman I'm interested in is you. It's always been you. Tad's parting words haunted her.

"No, don't say that," Casey said, smacking the mattress with her fist. "I can't let you hurt me again, Tad. I *won't* let you."

Forcing her thoughts back to André, she tried to drum up the memories they'd made together. It was disheartening to realize there weren't many. They both worked a lot, which was a lousy excuse, but the reality that she'd been denying wiggled its way to the forefront. Even when they were together, they didn't have much in common, and André somehow always finagled the restaurant into the conversation.

"We're going to make more time for each other and have some fun," she promised.

Once again, she tried to sleep, but rest wouldn't come.

Uninvited memories of the three years she and Tad had been together flashed through her mind like scenes from a movie. Talk about fun! The two of them had never stopped laughing. They'd known each other so well that they'd completed each other's sentences. Growing up on the lake had bonded them. They'd played, fought, and loved on Lake Tavadora. It was where they'd shared the most important moments of their lives, including talk of marriage and a family. Why had it all gone wrong?

Tears spilled from her eyes.

André had wanted to know if she still had feelings for Tad, and she'd answered with a resounding *No*. But if it was the truth, why did she feel guilty? Was she lying to him, *and* to herself?

CHAPTER SIX

That morning, Casey didn't get to the hotel until ten o'clock. When she rounded the corner and glanced at the lake, she was surprised to see a small group of people on the dock standing next to Tad's seaplane. Cupping her hand over her eyes to shade the glare from the sun dancing off the water, she realized they were all women. Tad was helping one of them into the plane. She couldn't believe her eyes. Obviously, he'd decided to go ahead and set up business. No doubt her father played a role in it.

How dare they both defy her!

As if he had extrasensory perception, Tad suddenly turned and looked her way. When he smiled and waved, she snorted out short breaths, feeling like a bull ready to rampage. Her feet stomped the grass as she disregarded the sidewalk and made an arrow straight across the courtyard lawn toward the pier.

Just as her feet hit the first wooden board, a hand touched her arm. Stifling a scream, she whirled. "Jack! You scared me half to death." So intent on her mission to stop Tad, she hadn't seen or heard the old man approach.

"Mornin', Casey." He tipped his captain's hat and then pointed to the end of the pier. "Tad is giving some of your guests a ride across the lake."

"I'll bet he is, and expecting me to pay him for doing so." Her heated gaze didn't waver from Tad, who was helping the last woman into the seaplane.

"Don't think so. If I were you, I wouldn't be so quick to stop him," Jack said.

Her head whipped around. "What do you mean?"

"Tad's not charging those ladies."

"Why not? That doesn't make sense."

"He's doing it as a favor to you."

Her gaze moved to Tad again, and she watched him climb into the plane. When the door slammed shut and the propeller started to turn, she muttered to Jack, "I don't get it."

He explained. "Those ladies saw the seaplane from the veranda and asked your front desk staff how they could get a ride. Having overheard them when he was eating breakfast in the tavern, Tad offered them a free ride, but there's a catch."

"What's the catch?"

"He made them each promise that they'd tell at least two of their friends about how wonderful the Lakeview Inn is and what a great time they had, as well as post good reviews on TripAdvisor." Jack grinned. "Apparently, those ladies agreed in a heartbeat. Tad does have a way with the ladies."

Despite herself, Casey couldn't help but smile. "Yes, he can be charming when he wants to be."

"Do you feel better now?" Jack asked.

"Huh?"

"You don't still want to kill him, do you?"

She playfully punched his arm. "Do you have a sixth sense, or something?"

He shrugged. "It's easy to spot a fire-breathing dragon."

She chuckled. "No, I won't kill him."

"Will you forgive him?" His gaze delved deep, causing the hair on her arms to stand on end.

"You're still talking about his giving rides without my permission, aren't you?" Why bother with the question when she suspected his inquiry had nothing to do with the plane ride.

"Might be, might not be," came his answer.

Just as she expected. Jack Butterfield was a man of mystery and riddles. She smiled and turned to leave. "Have a good day, Captain."

"You, too, Casey." Once she'd taken a few strides, he hollered, "Hey! Why don't you let me take the two of you out for a romantic boat ride tomorrow evening? Say, right before sunset? I won't accept any other reservations and it'll be my gift."

She halted, and her eyebrow lifted. It only took a moment for her to decide. She craned her head over her shoulder and replied, "That would be great. Thanks very much. André and I will be here around eight tomorrow night." She started up the walk to the inn, smiling, because, before she turned, she'd caught the surprised expression on Jack's face and heard him mumble, "Dang it."

****

"André, you told me your sous chef could handle dinner service tonight," Casey snapped, irritated that he was backing out on their sunset boat ride. She'd looked forward to their romantic date all day, and now he was cancelling. She wanted to slam the phone down, or better yet, smack him in the head with it. If only he were standing next to her. "Earlier this afternoon, you said there weren't many reservations and all the prep work was done for dinner."

"You know how it works, *mi amour*. This is my restaurant and my reputation on the line. One bad meal and I'm history."

"It's hardly that dramatic. No one has lost a restaurant because of one bad meal. And how do you think your sous chef feels? You're not giving him a chance to prove himself. There's no trust."

He sighed on the other end of the phone. "*Chez André* is my lifeblood. Please understand. We can do a silly boat ride anytime."

"But we don't," she countered. "I wanted tonight to be special. All we do is work. I really wanted to spend time alone together. We need it."

"If time alone is what you want, I'll come over to your bungalow when I close, and I promise you a night you won't forget." His voice growled with lust.

As recent as a week ago, she would have given in to that sexy French accent and agreed to see him later, but now, she just wanted to hit him with a blunt object. André thought sex was the answer to everything. After six months of giving and not receiving, she was realizing how selfish he was and wondering if the relationship would ever change.

Giving it one more Girl Scout try, she said, "Please. This means a lot to me. I'm sure your kitchen can do without you for one night."

"No, Casey." The gruffness in his tone startled her. "I said I can't go, so stop begging."

Her response cracked like a whip. "I'm not begging." Drawing in a ragged breath, she reached for calm. "Never mind. Forget it, André. I'll talk to you later." She ended the call, feeling her chest tighten.

"Knock, knock. Busy?" Her dad popped his head into her office.

"How long have you been standing outside?" she asked, sure he'd eavesdropped.

"Long enough to hear that André has disappointed you again." He sat in the chair across from her desk. "When are you going to realize that guy isn't for you, honey?"

"Dad, please. I don't feel like talking about this."

He held his hands up as if surrendering to the enemy. "Okay, okay. All I'm saying is there's a man around here who thinks the world of you. He's willing to do anything to get in your good graces again, and I think you ought to give him a second chance."

"Dad…" Casey shook her head.

"Have you heard about the free plane rides he's been giving to guests since yesterday morning?"

"I heard." According to Monica, more than fifteen people had taken Tad up on his deal, all promising to spread the word about the Lakeview Inn and write good reviews on the internet about their stay.

"He's doing it for you, to help drum up more business for us. And he hasn't asked for anything in return," Joe said.

"Except my forgiveness," she responded quickly.

He shrugged. "It's not much to ask. After all, it's been two years." His voice lowered. "Your mother wouldn't approve of you holding a grudge."

The ache she felt in her chest at the mention of her mom turned to a deep, agonizing burn. "That's not fair. You're playing dirty, Dad."

"Sorry, but you're a tough nut to crack. I have to pull out all the stops." When their gazes met, she graced him with a half-smile. "At the very least, you should thank Tad for what he's doing."

"A comped room for the week and docking his seaplane rent-free is thanks enough, in my book." She refreshed her computer screen. "Now, if you'll excuse me, I have a lot of work to finish before leaving today."

"Sure, kiddo." He stood to leave. "I happen to know Tad hasn't any plans this evening. Maybe he'd like to go on that boat cruise with you."

Her head jerked up. "How do you know about that?"

He grinned. "A little birdie told me."

"More likely, it was an old bird wearing a captain's hat. Can a girl not have any secrets in this town?"

"I don't think so, honey." Joe stepped through her office door and then popped his head back in. "Tad's having an iced tea and enjoying the view on the veranda right now, just in case you want to talk to him."

She grumbled, "Goodbye, Dad."

As soon as he was out of earshot, she gave Jack a call and cancelled the private boat cruise, offering to pay for the wages he was missing out on from having not taken outside reservations. She could forgive Tad for the hurt he'd put her through, but that didn't mean she wanted to start up again where they'd left off. There were too many unresolved issues and questions, and so far, he hadn't made an effort to explain himself. Although she'd tried to make herself believe she didn't care anymore, deep inside, she needed to understand why he'd left and why he'd broken off all contact after six months.

When she stepped out of her office and left through the back door, her body rocked with shock at finding him leaning against a live oak tree with his foot hiked against the trunk. Upon seeing her, he straightened.

"Evening, Casey. Heading home?"

"Yes." She continued past him at a quick clip. To her dismay, but not to her surprise, he followed.

"Can you slow down for a minute so I can talk to you?" he asked, keeping time with her long strides.

"I can't imagine what there would be to talk about, unless you're going to tell me you're checking out of the inn sooner than expected." She stopped, and her pulse started to race when their eyes met. "Is that it?"

"No. I mean, unless you need me to get out."

Her nose rode high in the air. "I told you, you can stay until Friday. That hasn't changed."

"Thank you."

She started walking again, and so did he.

"I was wondering if you'd have dinner with me tonight," he said.

Stopping again, Casey armored herself against the pull of his vibrant eyes. "I thought we agreed that seeing each other socially isn't a good idea."

"It was your idea, but I didn't agree."

"I have a boyfriend."

"And he stood you up tonight."

Her heart thundered inside her chest. "Who told…?" She struggled to tamp down her annoyance. "Of course. My father. He's rocketed straight up to the top of my list of people that deserve a kick in the pants."

When Tad laughed, the anger that had flashed so fast leaked from her as though someone had just pulled the plug in a bathtub. It had been so long since she'd heard his goofy laugh, a laugh that reminded her of the bray of a donkey. She hid a smile behind pursed lips.

"That's the old Casey I remember," he said. "You always say what you mean and mean what you say."

"What you see is what you get."

"And I like what I see. I always have." He took a tentative step closer.

"Stay where you are," she warned, placing a hand on his chest.

He grabbed her hand and held it tight. "Don't tell me the kiss we shared yesterday meant nothing to you."

"It meant nothing to me."

"Well, it meant the world to me. I'd been dreaming of kissing you for so long, you can't imagine. Since the moment I saw you again, I haven't been able to get you out of my mind."

Her nerves rippled beneath her skin. One moment she desired him, and the next, she wanted to throttle him for returning to Tavadora and causing her such angst. "What exactly do you want?" she asked, her shoulders sagging with fatigue.

His face drew close. "I want to take you to dinner, so I can explain."

"Explain what?"

"Why I'm here. I want to tell you what happened in Alaska and the reason I stopped communicating."

They stared at each other for what felt like a lifetime. Finally, she might find some closure. She was about ready to accept his invitation when he added, "You owe me that."

The comment felt like a punch to the stomach. He owed *her*; it wasn't the other way around. Incensed, she wriggled out of his grasp. "Think I'll pass. I've gone this long without knowing. What's another day, or two years?" She spun, her body shaking with fury.

"Wait. Where are you going?"

"Home. I'm gonna take a long, hot bubble bath. Then I'm gonna eat a quart of ice cream all by myself. And then, I might drink until I can't see straight."

Tad's eyes enlarged. "You never get drunk. Why would you want to do that?"

"How else am I gonna forget about all the selfish men in my life?"

His jaw dropped, and she left.

CHAPTER SEVEN

"Don't tell me you struck out again." Joe sighed.

Tad had run into Casey's father in the lobby. They treaded the stairs together, Tad heading to his room on the second floor and Joe to his suite on the third.

"I think I said something dumb," he admitted.

"She's not going to give you too many more opportunities to make things right," Joe warned.

"You're in the hot seat, too."

They stopped on the second floor. "What did I do?"

"You, me, and her deadbeat boyfriend are all on her crap list. She called us all selfish."

Joe's mouth turned down. "I never should have convinced you to come home. It's obvious that your showing up has caused her more pain. I betrayed my own daughter."

Tad clapped him on the shoulder. "It's not your fault. I pushed her too fast."

"That damn cook isn't making her happy either. I know if she gives you another chance, the two of you can work it out. Or, at least, be friends."

Tad shook his head. "I don't know. Casey's pretty upset right now. She probably never wants to speak to me again."

Joe looked into space. "I wouldn't blame her if she quit talking to me, too. Because of me, she had to give up her candy shop. I would have lost everything if

146

she hadn't sold it and took on the job of running this hotel. I'll never forgive myself for putting her in that position."

Tad's heart went out to him; he carried his own burden from having let Casey down. "Joe, I committed a worse crime. If I'd stayed and supported her instead of leaving to chase my own stupid pipe dream, everything would be different. My life…her life…We probably would be married today, maybe with a baby on the way. And my past wouldn't be haunting me."

Joe squinted. "Are you ready to tell Casey what happened in Alaska and why you wanted to come home for a fresh start?"

"I don't think she cares anymore."

Joe shook his head. "You know, even if you'd stayed in Tavadora, it wouldn't change the fact that I'm no businessman. I still might have run this place into the ground."

"Maybe, but I could have stepped in to help before it got that far. Casey could have kept her candy store. I take all the blame for what she's been through and for what she continues to go through. If only I could tell her how sorry I am."

"Me, too." He patted Tad on the arm and started up the next flight of stairs with his back hunched.

With nothing more to be said or done, Tad walked to his room, slipped the key in the lock, and plopped onto the bed with a heavy heart.

****

The next morning, Casey worked steadily to put out one fire after another around the hotel. Staying busy occupied her mind and kept her from thinking about Tad and André and how they'd both disappointed her.

It was close to one o'clock when she finally strolled to the kitchen to make a salad for lunch. Mable offered her a biscuit, which she accepted. "You know I can't say no to your biscuits," she complimented. "Dad, either. You probably have to hide them or he'll eat half the tray. How many biscuits did he woof down this morning with his coffee?"

"I haven't seen Mr. Walden this morning, Casey. Don't believe he's come down from his room yet."

A cold chill skated down her spine. Dad liked to sleep in, but never this late. And he never skipped breakfast or deviated from his daily routine. She set down her plate and rushed out of the kitchen.

A key to his suite was on her keychain, to use for emergencies, of which she determined this to be one. He could have had a heart attack or...No. She wouldn't let her mind go there. It had been just over a year since she lost her mom. She couldn't lose him so soon after.

The door clicked and she pushed it open calling, "Dad!" It only took a couple of minutes to search through the suite's four rooms. Relief settled upon her to know he hadn't fallen or was sick, but where was he? She slipped her cell phone out of her skirt pocket and punched his number on her contact list. After five rings, it went to voicemail, so she left a message. "Dad, where are you? I'm worried. Please call me as soon as you get this."

Once she'd relocked the door, she hurried down the stairs and asked Monica if she'd seen him.

"I've been swamped this morning, but now that you mention it, I haven't seen Mr. Walden. He usually says hello when he comes down the stairs, then he heads out to the veranda for breakfast."

"Call me on my cell if he shows up, will you?"

"Sure thing."

Trying her best not to overreact, she went out the front door and headed down to the lake, where she saw Jack talking to a group of people. She waited patiently on the grass as he described the tour they were about to take. Once he'd shown the last person onto the pontoon boat, he shuffled over to her. "Afternoon, Casey. What can I do you for?"

"Have you seen my dad today?"

"Yes, ma'am, I have."

Her eyes widened, and her hand flew to cover her heart. "Thank goodness. I thought he might be sick. Where is he?"

"He took a rowboat out early this morning. Said he had some thinkin' to do."

Relief was replaced by panic. Despite owning a hotel on the water, her father stayed as far away from water as possible. He'd never learned to swim and was deathly afraid of drowning. What on earth had possessed him to take a rowboat onto the lake?

"I can't believe it," she said. "He hates the water, and he's afraid of gators. Where would he have gone?"

"Don't rightly know, Casey, but I'm sure he's all right."

"How can you be sure?" she snapped and then immediately apologized. "I'm sorry, Jack. It's just that I'm worried. This isn't like Dad at all. I have no idea what has gotten into him lately, and this is utter foolishness to go off without letting someone know where he was headed."

"Maybe he told Tad." Jack nodded in the direction of the seaplane. Tad stood next to it, shining the wing with a rag.

"Yes, maybe he did. I'll go ask him. Have a nice cruise."

"It's gonna be a short one." He glanced into the sky. "Storm is comin'."

She looked up. It was blue and cloudless, but she'd learned long ago there was no point in disputing Jack. Sometimes she wondered if he had a crystal ball hidden under his cap that told him the future. "If you see Dad while you're out, will you please ask him to call me on my cell phone?"

Jack tipped his hat. "Will do, Casey. Enjoy your trip. I imagine it will be enlightening."

"Huh?" Jack and his riddles again. Ignoring the comment, she jogged across the beach and power walked down the long pier. She was out of breath by the time she reached Tad. His face broke into a wide grin upon seeing her, and he tossed the cleaning rag into a box.

"Casey! I've been thinking about you. I'm so glad you've given me another chance to explain."

"There's no time for that," she said, sharply. "Did you speak to Dad this morning?"

"No. I had breakfast alone. I haven't seen him today."

"What about last night?"

"Yeah, we talked for a few minutes before retiring to our separate rooms. Why? What's up?"

"For some reason, he took a rowboat onto the lake, but you know he's afraid of the water. This doesn't make any sense. Jack said he had things to think about, but what things?" She stared at the lake, as if the answer might lie somewhere within its depths.

Tad shifted from one foot to the other and shoved his hands into his jeans pockets. "I may know."

Her gaze snapped back to him. "Then tell me."

He relayed the conversation he'd had with her father the previous night. "He feels guilty for causing you to give up the candy shop. He probably just needed to get away for a while and brood."

A prickly feeling niggled beneath goose-fleshed skin. "Tad, I'm worried. He shouldn't be out there alone. He probably doesn't even have a life jacket on. Apparently, he's been gone for hours. He could be hurt or the rowboat could have tipped over. I don't think he knows how to row."

"And there's a giant gator in the lake, too."

"What?" She gasped as an image flashed through her mind of a gator eating her father.

A soft groan tore from Tad's throat. "Sorry, Casey. Forget I said that."

She nearly shrieked her response. "How can I?" She whirled to walk away. "I have to go find him."

He grabbed her arm. "We'll go together. It'll be quicker to take my seaplane. Joe should be easy to spot from the sky."

Casey didn't hesitate. She nodded firmly and planted her foot on the float and then stepped into the cockpit.

"Buckle up," he said, climbing into the pilot's seat. While he prepared to pull away from the dock, she texted Monica to let her know she would be gone for a while. Neither of them spoke while he taxied the plane further out.

As soon as he was on course, he opened the throttle and accelerated. When the plane lifted out of the water, Casey's stomach flipped and she squealed.

Tad chuckled. "You haven't ridden in a seaplane before?"

"No." She glanced out the window and looked back toward shore. "Oh. My. Gosh. The property looks so beautiful from up here. And the lighthouse!" She pointed to the old but still magnificent structure that had been so much a part of Tavadora's history, as well as the history of the Lakeview Inn. "The lake is so crystal clear and blue…" At a loss for how to express her feelings in words, her voice trailed off.

"If Joe's on the open water, we should be able to see him," Tad said.

"I hope he's okay. I can't imagine what possessed him."

For the next fifteen minutes, they both kept a watchful eye on the lake, but spotted nothing resembling a man in a rowboat. Just as Casey was beginning to feel very flustered, a voice cut through the air band transceiver.

"Jack, is that you?" Tad asked, speaking into the radio.

"Yes, Tad. Thought you'd want to know Joe is home, safe and sound."

Casey exhaled a relieved breath.

"Thanks, Jack. We appreciate you letting us know."

"No problem. I told Joe that Casey is with you. He says he's fine and for the two of you to enjoy the ride and take your time."

She rolled her eyes and chuckled. "I'm sure he did."

"Roger that," Tad said, smiling. "Over and out." He set the transceiver down. "What do you say? Now that you know Joe is safe, how about we take a longer ride over the chain of lakes?"

"Oh, I don't know. I really should be getting back to the hotel. I have so much to do, including chewing Dad out for causing me worry."

"Come on, Case. You're enjoying this, aren't you? Being up in the air?"

"Yes," she admitted.

"Okay then. You work so hard. Seems to me you deserve a little rest and relaxation, and the Lakeview Inn can do without you for another half hour. Sit back and enjoy the view."

"Well…" Before she could utter more, the plane swooped. She screamed and then laughed.

Tad glanced her way and their gazes caught. "You always did like a thrill."

It was better not to respond to that comment, as it could be taken in a couple of different ways, so she didn't.

She was thoroughly enjoying the flight when dark clouds suddenly blocked the sun. Within a matter of moments, angry-looking puffs blanketed the sky and rain began to fall.

"That came on fast," Tad said.

Casey's back went rigid. "Jack said a storm was coming, but it was clear as a bell when we left. You'd better turn back."

Rain began to pelt the plane harder, causing it to shake. The sound reminded her of rocks thrown into a whirling fan. She gripped the sides of her seat.

"Too late," he said. "I need to land. I'm not gonna take the chance of my plane becoming damaged or us getting injured."

"Where will you land?"

He pointed through the window shield. "There. Looks like a small island. We can take shelter there until the storm passes."

154

She nodded and gave his arm a little squeeze to let him know she trusted him.

He maintained a constant descent so that he could land the seaplane as near as possible to the shoreline. At the slowest speed, he approached the beach and then cut the engine. Once he steered it close enough, he jumped out, grabbed a rope and a knife from behind his seat, and splashed into the water to check the area for rocks or broken glass. Then he began to pull the plane in by hand.

The wind picked up and the rain was now falling in buckets, soaking Tad to the skin. He tailed the plane onto the beach. Then he cut the rope into pieces and secured the plane to attach points. Once he was satisfied it wouldn't drift away, he ran to the passenger side of the plane and hollered through the door.

"Behind your seat is a vacuum sealed bag. Grab it!"

Casey nodded.

Once she had the flat package in her hands, he gestured for her to exit. "Be careful." Just as the words left his mouth, she slipped on the wet float and plunged into his arms.

"Sorry," she muttered.

He hauled her up by the armpits and gripped her hand. Together they stepped off the float and ran for shelter beneath a canopy of trees with low-hanging branches. Amazingly, the coverage was so thick they barely felt the rain once they were underneath.

Both of them were wet, but poor Tad was drenched.

"Let me have that bag," he said. "There are two space blankets inside." He placed the package on the ground and sat on it to roll the air out. "There's one to sit on and one to keep us dry." He spread one of the blankets on the ground.

"Dry yourself off," Casey said, rubbing his wet hair with the blanket and then his body.

"Thanks. I'm fine. Let me dry you off so you don't catch a cold and get sick."

After he did so, they sat side by side, and she drew her legs up to her chest and wrapped her arms around her knees. When he draped the blanket around her head and shoulders, she insisted he share the warmth, swathing him in the other half. Fully aware of their bodies touching, old memories sprang into her mind of the years they'd spent together. Pleasant sensations ran through her torso, despite the terrible weather.

Once her teeth had stopped clicking together, she said, "I wonder how long the storm will last."

"You know Florida and its rainy season. This could go on for hours. Let's just hope there's no lightning."

As if the word itself was enough to conjure Mother Nature's temper, thunder boomed, sounding like a bomb had exploded. Casey jumped and snuggled closer to Tad. "That sure was loud."

"But no lightning," he stated. "We just might get lucky tonight."

"Tonight? You don't expect us to stay out here all night, do you?"

He shrugged and repeated, "You know Florida and its rainy season."

CHAPTER EIGHT

It had been two hours and the rain hadn't let up, though it was not coming down so hard anymore. Surprisingly, the space blankets kept them fairly dry and comfortable.

"Are you hungry?" Tad asked.

"Yeah. I didn't have lunch."

He dug into his jeans pocket and retrieved a stick of gum. "It's the best I can do, but it's all yours."

Smiling, Casey plucked it from his fingers, tore off the paper, and popped the gum into her mouth. "Thanks."

"You're welcome."

They'd been staring out of their makeshift tent to the churning water beyond and sharing small talk, mostly about the weather, but nothing deeper. Thrown together this way wasn't the scenario Tad had planned. Nevertheless, providence seemed to be working in his favor. What better place to beg forgiveness from the woman he loved than on a deserted island in the middle of a storm with no distractions?

Actually, it was the perfect scenario, especially since she seemed not at all interested in being combative. In fact, she'd smiled a few times, spoken pleasantly, and had even cuddled closer when it thundered. It was almost like old times.

Before he delved into what had happened in Alaska, however, he wanted to prove that he cared

158

about her life and happiness. After all, he did care. It wasn't B.S.

"How did you meet your boyfriend?" he asked.

Her head jerked toward him, and she squinted in suspicion. "Why do you want to know that?"

"There's no sign of the storm letting up, so we're stuck together. We may as well get caught up."

"That doesn't include talking about André," she said.

"Okay. Sorry I brought him up. Am I sensing he's a thorn in your side right now?"

"He's not a thorn in my side. It's just that my relationship is none of your business. The same as it's none of my business who you've had relationships with in the past eighteen months."

Tad's easy smile faded. "I haven't had any relationships since you. No dates even."

Her eyes widened. "That's a long time. I don't believe it."

"It's true. There's never been anyone else since we started going steady." His mouth tipped, hoping the use of the old-school term would de-ruffle her feathers that had suddenly ruffled.

It did. Casey returned the smile. A few beats passed before she spoke again. "Why? Weren't you attracted to Eskimo girls?"

Tad laughed out loud, pleased that she'd made a joke. The lift in her voice had him wondering if she was a bit jealous. Her gaze delved deep, and his thudding heartbeat drummed inside his chest.

His words rushed out like a waterfall. "I made a huge mistake leaving you, Casey. If I have to, I'll spend the rest of my life apologizing for being so selfish and stupid. I should have stayed in Tavadora. I knew how important that candy shop was. I left to chase my own dream, and I don't blame you for hating me for it." He gritted his teeth, ashamed.

Her gaze dropped to her lap for a moment before it returned to his face. She offered no consolation, but there were questions in her eyes.

The time had finally come. His story spilled out in a rush.

"You were right when you warned me not to trust Wade Gregory. I did partner with him in a hunting and expedition company, but as it turned out, that business was a front for his real trade, which was drug smuggling."

"Oh my gosh." Her jaw dropped.

"I won't go into all the gory details, but I do want to explain the reason I stopped communicating with you." His Adam's apple nervously slid up and down his throat. "When there wasn't a hunting trip scheduled, I flew to small towns all over Alaska making and picking up deliveries of all kinds. Wade made the arrangements and I did the flying. It was a way for us to bring in cash when the expedition business was slow. Unbeknownst to me, he was using me and my seaplane as a carrier for drugs on those trips. I swear I had no idea."

"What happened?" she whispered.

160

He cleared his throat. "Apparently, Wade had been on the FBI's radar for some time and they set up a sting operation. The trouble was, when he was busted, I was the person flying the plane with drugs on it."

Casey's hand flew to cover her mouth.

"I was arrested, tried as an accessory, and went to jail for a year. That's why I stopped calling, texting and emailing you." He hung his head. "I'd still be in jail today if it hadn't been for your dad."

"I don't understand."

Tad explained. "With Mom gone, I had no one to turn to. I was too ashamed to contact you and ask you for help, either financially or emotionally. I'd already let you down. There was no way I was going to put you in the middle of my problems, so I got in touch with Joe. He'd treated me like his own son since the day my dad left. He hired a lawyer and worked relentlessly to get me out of jail. It's because of him that I was finally released and cleared of the charges."

She was stunned. He could see it written all over her face.

"I can't believe Dad never told me. Did he ever travel to Alaska on your behalf?"

"Yes, he did. He visited me in jail and met with my lawyer several times."

She gazed into his eyes, her mind working. "He took several trips but never told me where he was going." She was thinking back and piecing a puzzle together. "It angered me that he was keeping secrets and left the inn to run itself. I didn't know if he'd met a

161

woman online that he was going to meet, or he was having a breakdown or a mid-life crisis of some kind. When he returned home from wherever he'd gone and I tried to pry information out of him, he shut me down." She sighed in disbelief.

"I'm so sorry we kept this from you. It killed Joe not to tell you, but I begged him. I was humiliated and embarrassed, and believe it or not, I was trying to spare you, in case you felt obligated to help. That was the last thing I wanted."

Puffs of air blew from Casey's lips, and he could tell she was holding in tears. "Did my father spend hotel money to pay for your legal fees?"

"What money I inherited from Mom was tied up in the business and my accounts were frozen when I was arrested. Selling my seaplane wasn't an option either, because it was held as evidence. Joe did help, but I honestly don't know where the money came from."

Her emotions exploded like a volcano. "Tad, how could you take advantage of him? And then you came back to Florida expecting him to give you a job? Hadn't he already done enough? You're not the man I used to know and love." Her gaze darted in all directions, like she was about to bolt, but the rain held her at bay. Instead, she scooted as far away from him as possible, which was only a couple of inches since they shared the blanket.

He reached for her hand but she withdrew it and stuck both hands under her legs. After several deep, cleansing breaths, he spoke sincerely. "Your dad is the best person I know. He insisted I come back home and start over again. Luckily, I was able to get my seaplane back, so yes, he did offer me a job at the Lakeview, but I didn't ask for it, and I turned him down several times before finally accepting. And I only accepted with the agreement that I work for free until my debt to him was paid off. Anything I earned from giving tourists rides was going straight back into his pocket. You put the kibosh on that plan, but I swear on my mother's grave that I'll find a job and pay him back every penny."

Casey's face twisted, and the dam finally burst. Tears splashed down her cheeks. "It's not necessary for you to swear on your mother's grave, Tad." When her head fell against his shoulder and she gulped back big sobs, he stroked her hair. "I had no idea," she hiccupped.

"I know."

"All this time, I thought you'd dumped me but weren't man enough to be honest and tell me."

"Oh, Casey."

"And I've been so angry with my father, too. I thought he'd mismanaged his money so badly, which is why I had to take over running the inn." Her sobs grew harder.

"I'm so sorry for hurting you," Tad whispered. "Tell me what to do to make it right. I'll do anything for you."

She shook her head. "Nothing can bring back what I worked so hard for."

"You can open another candy shop."

"No. It's too late for that. I'm stuck at the hotel for the indefinite future. And my hopes for marriage and family…" Her words stopped abruptly, and her tear-stained face lifted. Her wet gaze held him in an iron grip.

"You can still have that," he responded. His heart galloped, and he ached to kiss her, but a voice inside his head stopped him. He wouldn't have Casey accuse him later of having taken advantage of her, too.

"Of course I can," she choked, wiping her tears away with her hand. "André will make a great husband and father."

That wasn't the path Tad had hoped to go down, but Casey was a stubborn and proud woman. He knew when to push her and when to stop. It was time to stop and let her wrestle with her emotions, just as he continued to wrestle with his. The picture of her married to that French Canadian cretin made his blood boil.

She sat cross-legged and stoic, silently staring into the rain until darkness surrounded them and they both grew heavy with exhaustion.

At some point in the night, Tad woke. His back hurt from sitting straight up against a tree for so many hours, but the pain was worth it. No way would he move a muscle. Casey's head was in his lap, and the look on her face was that of an angel. She was right where she was meant to be, at least for a few more hours.

****

The next morning, Casey woke to birdsong, a clear sky, and calm water. Her entire body ached, and she felt chilled to the bone.

"The storm passed," Tad said. His fingers slid through the tangles of her hair. "We can go home now."

Realizing her head was lying in his lap, she rose to a sitting position, wondering how that had happened. *Got tired. Dropped off. And that's where I landed*, she surmised.

André's face flashed in front of her. What would he do or say when he found out she'd spent the night alone with Tad? Well, it wasn't as if they'd booked a room at the Marriott Grand Hotel and carried on a torrid night of romance. She rubbed sleep out of her eyes. Strange how the Marriott had popped into her head. Then again, maybe it wasn't so strange, because she and Tad had actually spent a romantic weekend at that hotel in Hilton Head for her birthday one year.

She glanced at him and he smiled, as if he could read her mind. It wasn't an altogether foreign notion, since they knew each other so well.

Pain sliced through her neck and down her shoulders. She winced. "I've got a crick in my neck."

"Let me rub it," he offered.

"No! Thanks," she added, politely. She didn't exactly feel guilty, because there was nothing to feel guilty about, but she was sure André would not appreciate another man rubbing her neck, especially the one man who had rubbed every part of her body in the past. "I'll be okay, but could you give me a hand up?"

"Of course." Tad stood and reached for her hand.

When they touched, a flame of desire sizzled through her. Their gazes latched, and his hand cupped her cheek. His touch felt good. It felt so right, and she wanted to kiss him more than anything, but there was too much water under the bridge. She'd spent such a long time angry with him. They could never go back to what they had before. Besides, André was waiting for her in Tavadora.

She gently pulled away. "Thank you for your promise to pay Dad back, and for telling me what happened. It was quite the bombshell, but now I have the closure I've desperately needed. I'm finally able to move on and put our relationship behind me once and for all."

His brows winged downward. "Closure? Move on? Casey, I was hoping this might be a new beginning for us. I was praying you'd be able to forgive me."

"I do forgive you, Tad, and the burden I've been carrying around has been lifted from my shoulders. Thank you so much for that gift."

"But…"

"But, we're not the same people as when you left. I've changed. You've changed, too. I wish you all the best, and I hope you wish the same for me."

He frowned. "If by *the best* you mean marrying that arrogant fool and raising a litter of snobby French

166

children, then the answer is no. That's the last thing on earth I wish on you."

"He's French *Canadian*."

"Whatever." Tad gathered up the space blankets and strode to the seaplane, kicking at fallen branches as he went. After throwing the blankets behind the seats in the cockpit, he hollered for her to jump in and started unknotting the ropes that had held the plane secure.

Surprised at his outburst, Casey climbed in without saying a word and snapped her belt buckle. Once he'd settled into the pilot's seat, Tad was all business. He sent a message to Jack by transceiver that they were returning to Tavadora, and then he taxied away from the beach. Not once did he make eye contact with her, not when they lifted off, and not when they were in the air.

No words were exchanged during the entire flight back.

Upon their smooth landing, Casey saw a small crowd of people standing on the dock, mostly employees of the inn. Front and center was her dad with André next to him. Tad must have noticed him, too, because he grumbled something under his breath and then said, "Wait inside until I get the plane secured."

Once it was safe for her to exit, Casey pushed the cockpit door open. With a few quick steps, Joe was there to help her out. They hugged and she whispered into his ear, "Tad told me everything, Dad."

He nodded and kissed her cheek. "I'm glad you're both home safe."

As soon as he released her, André stepped forward and grabbed her in a bear hug. In front of everyone, he gave her a long, lingering kiss. "I was so worried, *mi amour*. Are you all right?"

Embarrassed by the PDA, which was done in front of her employees and was not like André at all, Casey replied, "Yes, I'm fine. It was just a summer storm. We couldn't fly in the bad weather."

"Tad took very good care of her, I'm sure," Joe said, proudly, while shaking Tad's hand.

It was impossible for Casey not to see the dagger-like glares that flew between André and Tad.

"Well, the party's over now," she said, waving her arm in the air. "Back to work, everyone. As for me, I'm going home to take a hot shower, change my clothes, and then chow down on a big breakfast. I'm starving."

"I've got some fresh biscuits waiting for you," said Mable.

André's voice rose above the murmur of the crowd as they began to disperse. "Before you all go, there's something I'd like you to witness." He dropped to one knee and seized Casey's hand. "Casey Walden, the thought of losing you last night made me reevaluate my priorities, and I know now, more than ever, what is most important in my life, and it's you. You're the woman I want beside me now and always. Marry me."

Dumbfounded, her head grew light. Whether it was from lack of food, or the shock of his sudden, and not-terribly-romantic proposal, she wasn't sure. She

168

glanced at her dad. A deep crease cut across his forehead signaling his displeasure.

Maybe he was dehydrated, but when her gaze shifted to Tad, she could swear his face was white. She blinked her eyes. When they reopened, she knew it wasn't a hallucination. The depth of pain that filled his eyes cut her to the core.

André's slightly annoyed voice drew her attention back to him. "Casey, I'm waiting for your answer. What's the hold up? Don't embarrass me in front of all these people," he softly hissed.

Her head turned again to meet her father's cheerless gaze.

Unsmiling, Tad also stared, burning a hole straight through her.

Casey nibbled her lower lip. Finally, she quietly said to André, "Can I have time to think about it?"

The look he cast her was so cold, it felt like she'd been punctured by shards of ice.

He rose to his feet and kissed her knuckles in a show for those watching. "As you wish. There is no expiration date on our love. I'll drive you home now."

"Thank you, but I'd like my dad to drive me."

André's eyes enlarged. She sensed the fury beneath his calm demeanor at what he, no doubt, took as disrespect for not immediately accepting his proposal and then refusing his offer to take her home. He gave her a curt "goodbye" and strode up the pier.

Joe sidled next to her and looped his arm through hers. The crowd parted like the Red Sea as they walked toward the hotel. Once they reached the end of the pier, Casey glanced over her shoulder. Tad stood next to his plane with his arms crossed over his chest. She sensed a change in his demeanor, too.

Even from that distance, she saw him wink, and her heart skittered to a stop.

CHAPTER NINE

The next morning, Casey sprang out of bed, refreshed and full of life. She'd slept well, better than she had in weeks, and she'd had wonderful dreams, probably because she'd made a decision last night regarding André's proposal. Confident, she dressed quickly and called him. When it went straight to voice mail, she left a message.

"Good morning. I assume you're already at the restaurant, so I'll meet you there in thirty minutes to give you my answer."

Feeling like she was floating on clouds, she made the short walk to the inn, taking her usual route. This time, however, she didn't even look into the window of *Petite Sweets*. There were much bigger things on her mind.

Humming, she stopped when she saw a *For Lease* sign in front of the coffee shop across from the hotel. Rumor was it might be closing, but it was a shock to see that they'd already shut down and moved out. Guess she'd been too preoccupied for the past couple of days to notice. But notice now, she did. A pleasant thought rolled through her mind. *I have money in the bank from the sale of my candy store. If only…*

No. There was no point in thinking about it. Her dad still needed her. She cut across the street to the front of the Lakeview and waved at Jack, who stood on the dock in front of his pontoon boat with a large Styrofoam cup in his hand. Butch stood beside him with his tail wagging. Jack waved with his free hand.

Casey's gaze swung to the inn's pier, and she gasped. Where was Tad's seaplane? Suddenly, she remembered it was Friday. She'd told him earlier in the week he had to leave on Friday, but she didn't mean so early in the morning. Check-out wasn't until eleven o'clock. Hurrying up the front steps, she was about to pull the door open when someone called her name. Glancing to the left, she saw her dad at his usual table having breakfast.

"Good morning, sweetheart," he said, motioning her to join him.

"Good morning, Dad. Have you seen Tad?" Her brusqueness wasn't polite, but her stomach knotted with a sick feeling. "Have I missed him? Did he leave? His seaplane isn't at the dock."

"Slow down." Joe chuckled. "Sit and have some coffee."

"I don't have time. I just stopped in for a few minutes before heading over to see André at the restaurant."

He frowned. "Then I assume you've made a decision about marrying him."

"Yes, I have. I know you don't like him—"

Joe cut her off. "It's your life, honey. I've interfered enough as it is. I only want you to be happy. If you believe you can find it with that cook, then…you have my blessing."

She smiled. "Thank you, Dad. That means so much to me. Now, where is Tad? Do you know?"

"He moved his plane over to the marina. He promised to check out as soon as he returns from signing a lease for a boat slip."

"Oh, shoot."

"What's wrong?"

"I'm glad he didn't fly away, but I didn't expect him to go rent a slip so quickly."

Joe tilted his head. "Fly away? Where would he go, honey? This is his home, and he's here to stay."

Home. The word conjured up warm memories again.

"Tad told me about his agreement with you, about working here for free until he pays you back. It's important that he keeps his promise. He needs to stay." She glanced at her watch. "Maybe I can stop him from signing a contract if I get to the marina in time."

"Are you sure about this, Casey? I really never expected to get the money back. I just had to help him. I hope you can understand that."

"I do, and you did a great thing for him, but I know Tad would never take advantage of your generosity. He wants to do right by you." Her head was swimming. "I need to check on a few things inside before I go over to *Chez André*, but I also want to stop Tad from signing a lease." Torn about which to do first, she quickly made her decision. "I'm going to the marina before I do anything else." Her heart pounded with an insane rhythm. What she had to say to both men would change her life forever.

"Honey, before you go, there's something I want to tell you."

"What is it, Dad?"

He glanced over his shoulder. "Did you happen to notice the sign in front of the coffee shop across the street?"

"As a matter of fact, I did. I didn't know they were moving out so fast. Wonder what will be going in there."

He grinned like a Cheshire cat. "Casey's Candies."

"What are you talking about?"

"I met with the owner of the building last night, Parnell Harper, and the place is yours to lease, if you want it."

She didn't comprehend. "That was sweet of you to meet with him, but I can't leave the inn. You need me."

He shook his head. "No, I don't. Well, I take that back. I will always need you, but as my daughter, not as the manager of my hotel."

"Huh?" Her head angled in confusion.

"I'm going to be taking a more active role again, but don't worry. I'll have the help of someone very experienced in the hospitality industry to keep me on track."

"Who would that be?"

"A lovely woman by the name of Alice Cavanaugh. She's a widow, currently living in Orlando. Alice was married to a man whose ancestor, Linus Cavanaugh, had ties to Tavadora and the lighthouse across the lake in the early nineteen hundreds. She and her husband ran a very successful bed and breakfast for twenty-eight years. When I made up my mind that it was time to relieve you of your obligation here at the inn, I started making contacts with people in the business, and someone recommended Alice. She and I met recently. We really hit it off, and she's very excited to move to Tavadora and come onboard. I have her resumé in my room for you to look at. You'll see she's going to be a perfect fit."

Casey's eyebrow arched. Her father seemed a little too excited about handing over the reins to a stranger. "Will she be a perfect fit for the hotel or you?"

His eyes twinkled mischievously. "Maybe both. No one will ever replace your mother, but Alice is a very nice lady."

"Dad! I can't believe you've made another decision without consulting me first." She wasn't sure whether to be annoyed or relieved.

He stood and hugged her. "I'm doing this for you. I don't have the money to put into a new store, but I'll release you from the burden of managing *my* dream, and I'll provide sweat equity and emotional support to help you get yours back. I was thinking you might have the cash flow to get a new shop up and running."

"I do."

"Then please accept my gift graciously. You deserve your dream, and you're going to have it."

Her throat clogged with emotion. "Are you sure?"

"One hundred percent."

She wrapped her arms around him and cried, "Thank you so much."

"Does that mean you're going to contact Parnell and sign a lease?"

"After the trouble you've gone to, how can I not?" Her life was changing in so many ways in such a short time. She looked at her watch again. "I need to go see André, but I want to talk to Tad first."

"Lucky for you, he's saved you a jog to the marina." Joe grinned and gazed over her shoulder.

Casey spun, and her hand fluttered at her chest. "Tad! Did you sign a lease for a boat slip at the marina?" Before he could answer, she babbled on. "Dad and I want you to stay on and give rides over the lake just like you and he planned. Remember, you have a promise to keep. If you go back to the marina and explain, I'm sure they'll let you out of the lease."

Tad stepped close, and the scent of his cologne made her dizzy with longing.

"I can't do that, Casey."

"Why not?" Her stomach clenched.

"Because I didn't sign a lease to rent a boat slip. I was at the marina to talk to someone about purchasing my seaplane."

"Why?"

"So I can support you. My plan was to use the money to help you open a new candy shop."

He could have knocked her over with a feather. "That *was* your plan? You say it in the past tense."

"Yes. The guy changed his mind. I'll find another buyer," he added quickly.

Her voice faltered. "You were willing to sell your plane for me?"

He moved closer and placed his hands on her hips. They were so strong and comforting. "I told you, I'd spend the rest of my life doing what was necessary to make up for the pain I caused. I will, and that's a promise. I've already got a couple more leads that I'm going to contact today."

She shook her head and smiled. "You don't have to do that."

"It's taken care of," Joe piped up. "I've already arranged for Casey to lease the coffee shop across the street for her new candy store."

The genuine smile that stretched Tad's lips was so wide it could have slid off his face. "Are you kidding?"

"That's not something I'd joke about, son," Joe said.

Casey affirmed by fervently nodding her head.

"So, I can work here until I pay off what I owe you, Joe?"

"I hope you'll stay even after the debt is paid. My guests have been asking me when the handsome young pilot is going to be open for business, especially the ladies."

Casey chuckled and lightheartedly punched Tad's shoulder. "You'd better get your seaplane back to the dock ASAP and hang your shingle out. You don't want to keep the ladies waiting."

When their laughter ebbed, Tad said, "Casey, there's something I want to say."

Her heart began to hammer. "There's something I want to say, too."

"Time for me to leave," Joe said.

"You can stay," the couple replied in unison. They stared into each other's eyes, and Casey's lips parted in a smile.

"We always did finish each other's sentences," Tad said.

She palmed his clean-shaven cheek. "Then finish this one. I…"

"Love you."

She felt electricity surge between them as his arms encircled her.

"I love you, Casey. I always have and I always will. You can't marry that other guy."

She shook her head. "No, I can't. I'm telling him this morning. You're the only one for me." Her fingers trailed through Tad's golden locks.

"Yahoo! You're going to be my son after all." Joe clapped Tad on the back and gave Casey a kiss.

"Slow down, Dad," she warned. "Tad didn't ask me to marry him."

"Not yet, but first comes love, then comes marriage, then comes a baby in a baby carriage." He winked and left to go inside so they could have privacy.

"It doesn't rhyme, but somewhere in that lineup comes the candy shop," Tad joked.

Casey tossed her arms around his neck. "I don't care in which order they fall, Tad Singer. Together, we can weather any storm. We're going the distance this time, and I look forward to taking the ride with you."

Part III

JACK'S STORY

(*The Future*)

Stacey Coverstone

CHAPTER ONE

Winter, 2120
Tavadora, Florida

Jack Butterfield was dying. So was Butch, his Jack Russell dog, who had been his faithful companion since 1910.

The two lay shivering on Jack's single bed, both covered with a blanket. Butch was curled next to Jack's body in the crook of his arm.

"Butch is cold," Jack said.

Although it was over 100 degrees outside and Naomi Dunn, his nurse, was in the throes of menopause and experienced hot flashes off and on every day, she tossed a few twigs into the ancient wood stove that Jack had stubbornly refused to junk. No one had used wood as fuel for over fifty years, but he insisted the old ways were better.

"I see him trembling, poor thing," she answered sweetly, while wiping her face with a tissue and pulling her damp hair into a ponytail at the back of her head. She gave the sizzling embers a stir with a poker before shutting the cast iron door.

It was her job to show kindness, compassion, and consideration to her patients, no matter what was requested of her. That didn't mean Jack took advantage of the woman, who was not only his neighbor, but also his friend. However, Butch deserved to leave this world with as much comfort and ease as possible. He'd been Jack's best buddy for 210 years.

"I love that dog, too," Naomi said, settling her bulk into a chair next to the bed. "Whatever he needs, I'll take care of it. The same goes for you. Hold your arm out." She withdrew a medallion-shaped piece of metal from her medical bag and tried to press it into Jack's arm to take his blood pressure, but he gently swatted at her hand.

"You can put that thing away, Naomi. Don't need to know what my vitals are. They're not good. We both know I'm in my final hours."

She frowned. "I wish you wouldn't talk like that, Jack. There's always hope."

He shook his head. "The end has finally come for me and Butch. We're not long for this world." He forced a smile through dry, cracked lips.

In a short seven-day period, his body had gone downhill faster than the drone Naomi's grandson rode through the neighborhood. He'd physically regressed from a vibrant 61-year-old to a frail, weak, shell of a man. His muscles were now atrophied. His strong back felt as brittle as a dry branch. Most of his silver hair had fallen out to leave only a few sad strands across the top of his scalp, and his once piercing blue eyes had grown dull the last time he looked in the mirror.

Butch whimpered. Jack rubbed under the dog's fully grayed chin with his finger. Staring at him blankly were eyes that had only recently sparkled with fun. "It won't be long before we take the last train to glory, boy." Jack turned his head. "Naomi, will you please give Butch a drink?"

"Of course, hon." She siphoned some water from the pitcher sitting on the bedside table into an eye dropper and shuffled to the other side of the bed. "Here you go, Butch." Gently, she opened his mouth and squeezed water into it. He licked his lips and closed his eyes.

Naomi returned to her chair and took a long gulp from her can of soda. Jack could tell she was hotter than blazes, but the dear woman didn't complain.

"Are you sure you don't want me to call the vet, Jack? I'm sure he could do more for little Butch than I can. He can heal bodies with technology. Just last week he brought Penny Hanson's deceased cat back to life with that laser gun of his."

He reached to pat her hand. There was hardly any strength left to do much more. "You're handling things just fine, Naomi. There's nothing any doctor can do, but I appreciate your concern. You're the one we want taking care of us in these, our final moments."

She smiled and nodded.

His mouth was parched. "Water, please," he wheezed.

She rose and filled a glass with water from the pitcher and then lifted his head with her hand so that he could drink. When he'd guzzled all he could without choking, he said, "Tavadora sure has changed since the lake dried up and became a desert thirty years ago, hasn't it?"

"Yes, it has," she agreed, solemnly. "The temperatures have continued to steadily rise, and there are no green spaces anymore, only dirt and sand. All of our once abundant citrus groves are long gone. Those who earned a living from the lake had to move on years ago. I know you were once a fisherman, Jack."

He nodded. "I've fished all my life. I also conducted boat tours around the lake and through the canal, gave diving lessons…" His voice drifted off for a moment. "The lake always provided for me." He thought back to the days when he lived and worked on beautiful Tavadora Lake. Those times were long gone, as were loved ones, friends, and places that had meant so much to him.

One such landmark that held a special place in his heart had started out in the late 1880s. It was called the Lake House then, a simple but charming ten-room hotel on the water. By the early 21st century, the property had morphed into three separate buildings, and the popular resort changed its name and was known as the Lakeview Inn. However, as more years passed, the already old hotel continued to deteriorate from age and weather. Several businesses tried, but failed, to maintain it as a historic attraction before a hurricane completely destroyed the entire estate in 2068. Only a plot of dirt remained to this day.

Naomi continued to reminisce about the state of things in Tavadora. "I was in high school when the city council decided to re-route a major thoroughfare through town. That sure didn't help our economy. It destroyed what little charm was left and tourism dwindled. Then, when that giant sinkhole swallowed up most of downtown fifteen years ago, the tourists stopped coming altogether."

"It once was a boom town," Jack said. "But nearly everyone except a few of us staunch locals stayed after the sinkhole incident. There were hardly any outsiders moving in by that time, anyway."

"When I was a little girl, my grandparents would tell me stories about how the entire state of Florida used to be a major tourist attraction," Naomi said, shaking her head."They showed me old photos of a place called Disney World that used to be in Orlando. They said people came from around the world to visit."

Jack clearly remembered Disney World. He'd even been there one time. What had once encompassed 40 square miles was now another dried-up patch of ground, and had been for decades.

Naomi sighed, dreamily. "I've always been fascinated by the history of Tavadora. I've read that a few brave families settled the area over two hundred years ago and it eventually grew into a charming, unique, and very pretty town. Folklore has it that some claimed Lake Tavadora emitted some sort of power that drew people to it. I sure wish I'd lived back in those days." She gazed at Jack. "You've been here quite a few years, so you got to experience some of the good times. Am I right?"

Jack squinted, deciding then and there that he would not go to his grave without someone knowing

Lake Tavadora (The Trilogy)

that Lake Tavadora *had* held magical powers. He cleared his throat. "Naomi, it's important to me that someone know my story. I have no family, and you're about as good of a friend as I have, so I want to tell it to you, before I go."

"Well, sure, Jack. I'll listen," she said, plumping his pillow and helping him to sit up a little straighter.

He kept his arm snuggled around Butch. "This won't be any run of the mill yarn, Naomi. This is the story of my life, and the things I have to say might come as a shock."

She smiled, and he supposed in her line of work she'd heard a lot of tales, some of which may have been exaggerated or embellished by sick people talking out of their heads. Nurses were trained not only in medicine, but also in counseling, which meant being a good listener. But she hadn't heard anything like what he was about to tell her, of that he was certain.

"I'm ready when you are," she said, leaning forward with her elbow propped on her knee and her fist under her double chin. "I love a good fable, and we have all afternoon."

"I'm not sure about that," he mumbled. "Anyway, my life started in Pittsburgh, Pennsylvania where I was born and raised. But when I was thirty-one years old, my bride, Maisie, and I grew tired of the harsh winters and made our way to this part of central Florida, which was just a fledgling settlement at the time. The year was *eighteen eighty-one*." He emphasized those last words and then stopped and stared at Naomi.

Her brows furrowed and she angled her head. It seemed her mind was working. She counted on her fingers. Suddenly, her jaw dropped. "Hold your horses, Jack. Are you sure you've got that year right?"

"Yes, ma'am, I do."

"But how can it be? That would make you...you..." She countered her fingers again.

He mustered a smile. "I'm two hundred and sixty-six years old. Butch is a fifty-some odd years younger, just a whippersnapper."

Her eyes narrowed playfully, probably thinking he was joshing her. "Impossible. No one lives that long, even with today's medicines."

"Not impossible," he assured, with a straight face.

"I'm listening." She grinned, obviously playing along to oblige an old man.

He scratched Butch's head and replied, "It was the lake. There was magic in those waters."

CHAPTER TWO

"Imagine following a potholed path through thick woods and coming upon a shimmering body of water gleaming in the distance," Jack said. "Such was the case when Maisie and I drove our wagon into the settlement that we soon learned was called Royalview. The year was eighteen eighty-one, and only a handful of families had homesteaded the area at that time. I recall those folks well. Dudley Adams, David and Mary Simpson, the Longstreet family, J.P. Donnelly, and Dora Drawdy, who died a couple of years after Maisie and I arrived, are a few that come to mind. Dora and her husband, Jim, had moved to Florida back in eighteen forty-six and established a squatter's homestead several miles south of the town."

He smiled at the memories. "Our first glimpse of Lake Tavadora was of mist rising from the water, trees draped in Spanish moss, marshy grasses, and a sandy shore. After living in the city, Maisie and I thought we'd died and gone to heaven. It didn't take long for us to find our plot of land and for me to put up a simple dwelling. Our first home was a log cabin, same as everyone else's, and we had no indoor plumbing." He chuckled, remembering the many times he'd shared an outhouse with lizards and snakes.

"Didn't Maisie mind?" Naomi asked, getting into the story.

He shook his head. "My Maisie was a strong and brave woman. She had to be, in order to leave the big

188

city and follow me to a new and strange land. She was smart, too. Public education was established the same year we settled here, and she became the school teacher."

"What class did she teach?"

"Back then, all the ages were taught together in one room. She loved the children and taught them all."

"Did you fish for a living?"

"Yep. Right from the start, I earned our livelihood from the lake. Farming or harvesting timber wasn't for me, nor was working the citrus groves. Maisie had wanted me to purchase a grove when we first got here, but I refused. I like the water and was drawn to it as if I'd been born a fish. When all the groves froze a few years later, many people were wiped out financially and had to leave. When that happened, Maisie told me she was glad I'd been a stubborn old mule. By that time, we were making ends meet just fine, and we were content. She'd grown to love our life here and would have been heartbroken if we'd had to leave our home and the thriving community."

Jack paused and asked for another sip of water. He drank, stared at Butch for a moment, and then continued. "Those early years were happy ones. We worked hard, and the town grew rapidly. The name changed to Tavadora, and we all enjoyed the benefits that came from more families moving in and businesses growing.

J.P. Donnelly was one of the town's wealthiest citizens. He donated land for the first two churches to be built on, a lot for the fire department, and acreage for the cemetery. We also had a drugstore, a grocery, Mr. True established a general store, and the Englishman George Booth and his wife opened a hardware store. Steamboats brought commercial goods into Tavadora until the arrival of the railroad in eighteen eighty-seven. In the beginning, only one train came and went each day, carrying freight, mail, and passengers. The times were quite exciting."

Naomi chuckled. "I remember reading about trains in History class at school. My, my, but train transportation sure was a long time ago. I would have liked to ride on one, but I suppose they were quite slow."

"Yes," Jack agreed. "A train moved like a turtle compared to the drones and the flying vehicles that now carry us through the air at speeds of one hundred miles per hour."

Naomi grinned. "We've been friends for several years, Jack. Be honest with me. I like a good yarn as much as anyone, but you've got to be pulling my leg about having lived back in the eighteen hundreds. I don't mean to hurt your feelings, but it simply cannot be true."

He made a cross over his heart with his finger, and his mouth drew into a thin line. "I know it's got to be the most incredible thing you've ever heard, but have you ever known me to lie about anything since you've known me?"

She didn't hesitate. "No. You're the most honest man I know."

He nodded, firmly. "I swear on my dear wife's grave that I'm telling the whole truth and nothing but the truth." Swearing on a loved one's grave was not something to be taken lightly in their neck of the woods.

Their gazes fused and she clapped a hand over her mouth. "You old son of a gun, you're not lying!"

"No, I'm not."

"I…I…don't know what to think about this," she stuttered. "What am I *supposed* to think?"

"You don't have to think," he replied. "Just listen." He breathed in and out deeply, feeling his lungs constrict. "I don't have much time and I want to get it out."

"Let me call the doctor," she begged. "He can do more than me." She jumped up from her chair, but his skinny arm thrust out, and his fingers gripped her wrist.

"You're giving me all I need. Please let me finish my story before it's too late."

With sympathy in her eyes, she nodded.

"Life was not all work," he continued. "Maisie and I enjoyed a social life that revolved mostly around religious and community-oriented activities. But sometimes we took walks in the woods together or we'd find a quiet spot to have a picnic lunch. She loved for me to take her down the canal in my rowboat. She sure did enjoy spotting the shorebirds."

"Sounds like you were quite the romantic."

Jack sighed. "My romantic side was only for her. I would have done anything for that woman. We had twenty-nine blissful years together before it was over."

Naomi was too polite to ask why the marriage hadn't lasted longer. She probably figured he'd get to that part of the story when he was ready.

He shifted his body a bit to make breathing easier. It felt like a brick was lying on his chest. When he moved, Butch grunted but kept his eyes closed.

"Is there something else I can do to make either of you more comfortable?" Naomi asked.

"No thanks. We're as good as can be expected. Now where was I?"

"You had twenty-nine beautiful years with your wife."

"Oh, yes. Let me tell you how this old dog was lucky enough to marry that sweet gal."

"Please do."

"I was thirty years old and a confirmed bachelor. It wasn't that I didn't like women, because I did. I liked the fairer sex a little too much, you might say. I was what they called a playboy in those days." He chuckled. "I never imagined settling down with just one lady. There were so many pretty blondes, brunettes and redheads everywhere you turned. I didn't know how a man was supposed to choose, so I decided not to, but fate has a way of playing with a fella."

Naomi's eyes twinkled with curiosity. "How did fate play with you, Jack?"

"I was working for an iron and steel-related manufacturer in Philly at the time. The job was so boring it was about to kill me, so when my buddy Frank invited me to travel with him and his two sisters to Ocean City, New Jersey to attend the wedding of a family friend, I jumped at the chance. My only obligation was to act as an escort to one of Frank's sisters. Best decision of my life."

"Because you met Maisie at the wedding," Naomi stated.

"Yep. A sprightly young lady in an emerald green gown crossed my path that summer day, and I was forever changed." He closed his eyes as the vision of the blonde-haired, violet-eyed Maisie filled his mind.

"She was a mature young woman for only twenty-four. She also was straightforward, saucy, stunningly pretty, and strong-willed, as I'd soon come to learn. After the wedding ceremony was over and everyone was enjoying the reception, I noticed that Frank's sister, whom I was supposed to be escorting, had taken a fancy to the bridegroom's brother. I didn't mind, as her departure left me free to relax and not worry about being on my best behavior. My gaze wandered around, flitting over the crowd of partygoers. That's when I saw her."

Jack smiled. "She was standing across the lawn staring at me. Very bold behavior, for the time period," he assured. "I smiled and lifted my glass as a sort of toast. She lifted her glass and returned the smile. Before we knew it, we found ourselves escaping the party and walking the nearby beach together, talking and laughing and digging holes in the sand. At one point, we stumbled across an abandoned rowboat, which we quickly decided was ours for the taking. It was to be the first of many boat rides. Oh, what a happy day it was."

"Did you fall in love at first sight?" Naomi wanted to know.

He nodded. "It was quick and easy for us both. I guess you could say we swept each other off our feet. I knew that very day that she would become my wife. When I returned to Philly, we wrote letters to one another and came to an understanding within a few weeks. Though I broke free to visit New Jersey when my work would allow, our courtship was mainly by correspondence.

While conforming to the ritual of the day, our engagement lasted close to one year. We wrote letters two or three times a week during that period, and I often found myself chasing a mail wagon to the train station after dark and spending extra for special delivery. You see, long distance telephone calls lay a good distance ahead. Years later, Maisie joked that no one who ever had to depend on the railroad for their love would call that road smooth."

Naomi's cheeks warmed to a pretty pink and she sighed, perhaps thinking back to her own courtship with her husband who had died a few years earlier.

"The day I married that girl was the best day of my life," Jack said.

"And she left New Jersey to live with you in Philadelphia?"

"Yes, but after one winter together, we made the decision to leave. Aside from the cold and snow, Philadelphia was dull and its citizens even duller. Most seemed content with the city's lack of change, but not me and Maisie. We both had adventure on our minds and in our souls."

"So you headed to Florida."

"We headed to Florida, the land of sunshine and palm trees. We forged a good life together for twenty-nine years, and then the sunshine left my life."

"What happened, if it's not too painful to talk about?"

"She died of an infection." Even after all these years, the recollection of her loss caused his chest to burn with an agonizing ache. "If only the medical community knew back then what they do today, or even a hundred years ago. I'm sure she could have been saved."

There was a catch in Naomi's throat when she responded. "I'm so sorry, Jack. You never remarried?"

He shook his head. "There was no one that ever came close to making me feel the way my Maisie did."

"And you two never had children?"

"No, we were not blessed, but I was a godfather to a beautiful girl named Blanche. She died in nineteen thirty-five. I still miss her."

Silence stretched between them until Butch squirmed and opened his eyes. A whine brought Naomi to her feet. She filled the eye dropper again and inserted it into Butch's mouth. He licked his lips and offered her a weak blink before falling back to sleep.

"Butch sure is a special dog," she said, stroking his weak body.

"Yes, he is," Jack said. "This little man is my best friend, and it's time to tell you how the two of us met."

CHAPTER THREE

"I was in pretty bad shape when Maisie died," he related. "She was everything to me and then suddenly she was gone. I had my work to distract me during the day, but the nights were the worst. Loneliness is a terrible thing."

Naomi nodded in agreement. Jack was sure she knew the feeling since she'd lost her spouse.

"Anyway, I started taking a few nips from a whiskey bottle each night to help me take my mind off of the sorrow. I hadn't been much of a drinking man before, but within a short time, I found myself hooked to the poison. As soon as I got home from fishing, I sat in my chair and took to the bottle. Most nights I fell asleep in the chair and woke with not only a hangover, but also a crick in my neck. One evening I ran out of whiskey and wasn't ready to call it a night, so I stumbled to town in search of the only thing that settled my mind."

He shifted his body because one hip had grown numb. When Butch squeaked in protest, Jack tenderly slid a hand under his body and moved the dog higher up on his chest. "Now he can feel my heart beating, slow as it is."

"What more can I do to make you comfortable?" Naomi asked. Her face pinched with concern.

"Another drink will suffice, please." Although he knew he'd be going to his reward within hours, there

197

was no fear. In fact, after all these years, death was welcome, but not before his entire story had been told.

She lifted the glass to his lips and he swallowed, feeling a bit lightheaded. "Thank you, Naomi. Where was I?"

She set the glass on the bedside table and repositioned herself in her chair. "You went to town for more whiskey."

"Right. I'd just gotten to Mr. True's general store when I heard a ruckus from around back."

Naomi leaned forward. "What kind of ruckus?"

"Laughter and yelping."

"Yelping?"

He felt his eyes grow dark at the recollection. "When I turned the corner, what I saw made me madder than a wet hen."

"What did you see?"

"A couple of kids were kicking at something on the ground. The thing was alive and it was crying bloody murder. As I drew closer, I saw that the thing was a little dog."

Naomi's gaze darted to Butch resting on Jack's chest. She worried her bottom lip between her teeth. "It was Butch."

"Yes," Jack replied, solemnly. "My blood began to boil, and boy, did I sober up fast. Without thinking— just reacting—I strode toward those two boys and grabbed them both by the shirt collars and swung them around like rag dolls. Their eyes nearly popped out of their heads when I tossed them on the ground and bellowed a few choice words. It was the one and only time I felt murderous." His eyes narrowed. "You see, I can't stand to see an innocent animal harmed."

"Me either," Naomi said, clenching her hands into fists. "Did the boys run away?"

"You bet they did, but not before I gave them each a boot in the pants so they'd know how it felt to be abused. They were lucky that's all they got, the way my temper sparked. As they ran, I hollered after them that I knew where they lived and who their parents were, and if I ever saw or heard of them doing harm to another animal, they'd pay a heavy price. And I meant it."

A smile crept into Naomi's face. "You were one tough son of a gun, eh, Jack?"

"So I've been told." He pushed out a grin and then turned serious again. He gently stroked Butch's ear. "The poor little fella was shaking with fear, and when he tried to move, he limped and cried. It 'bout broke my heart."

"His leg was broken?"

"I wasn't sure. When I went to pick him up he didn't squeal, so I did so gently, and the moment his big eyes looked into mine, I knew we were going to be the best of pals. I took him to the animal doctor, and as it turned out, the leg was only sprained and his ribs were bruised. Doc guessed he was about four or five years old at the time. I named him Butch after my little brother who died when we were kids. I took him home and nursed him back to health, and we've been together ever since."

He scooted the dog up close to his face and kissed the tip of his cold nose. "This little man is the reason I was able to stop my destructive behavior that surely would have been my ruin. I had someone to care for again and to take care of, so I promised to quit drinking that same night and haven't had a drop since." He turned to stare at Naomi when he heard her sniff.

She wiped a tear from her eye. "Oh, Jack, that's the sweetest story. I know I've never seen the two of you apart."

"We've lived more than twenty decades together."

She angled her head. "About that…"

"Are you still wondering if I'm a senile old man off his nut?"

"No, the whole thing does seem improbable, but I do believe you. I'm just twitching with nerves. I can hardly wait to know how it happened."

"Do you mean the miracle?"

"Yes."

"Then I'll tell you."

Just then Naomi's hand went to her ear and she gently squeezed on her ear lobe. "Excuse me, Jack. I have a phone call."

"No problem. Go ahead and take it."

She spoke. "Hello." After a moment of listening, she said, "Are you sure it can't wait?" Then she grumbled, "Oh my gosh. Okay. I'll be right there." With another squeeze to her lobe, the call was ended. "That was my grandson. I have to run home, but hopefully I won't be long. Will you be all right if I leave you for a few minutes?"

Jack didn't fear dying alone, because Butch was with him, and the longer the pain surged through his body, the more he wanted his physical life to finally be over. But he was determined to complete the telling of his story so that someone realized how special Tavadora and the lake had once been. Because he'd seen so many changes in his lifetime, he hoped humanity could learn from his experiences. Perhaps better decisions could be made for the future, based on the simpler lifestyles of the past.

"Take care of business and hurry back," he said.

She stood up. "I promise."

After the front door shut behind her, he closed his eyes and let this thoughts drift. Technology, among other things, sure had changed drastically. He'd been born before Alexander Graham Bell invented the telephone, but he clearly remembered when the news of that miracle machine went around the world.

The candlestick phone came next, becoming popular in the 1890s. Jack recalled the amazement on Maisie's face the first time she spoke into one of those contraptions. In the 1930s, manufacturers combined the mouthpiece and receiver into a single unit. Then came the rotary phone, tedious to use, he recalled, followed by the modernized push-button phone.

Portable phones were invented in the 1980s. Although they could weigh up to 1.75 pounds, Jack remembered the excitement of being able to talk anywhere in your house because there was no cord attached. Then, in the late 1990s, a flip phone was introduced, weighing a mere 3.1 ounces.

At the start of the 21st century, phones included a camera. Soon, smartphones, with their intuitive touch screens, intelligent sensors and sleek designs, were introduced to the masses. Around 2030, smartphones evolved into wearable devices, providing a constant stream of advertising and programming directly into the user's vision.

Twenty-five or so years later, wrist phones were up and coming, and they were customized to fit each person's arm perfectly and included state-of-the-art voice command features as well as a holographic feature that allowed people to chat with friends and family as if they were sitting right beside them.

About 65 years ago, technology took a giant leap with microchips being installed in every phone user's brain. Now, thoughts connected instantly when people dialed to call each other. You squeezed on your ear lobe to connect and squeezed again to disconnect.

He sighed, knowing he was the only man on earth to have experienced such incredible change.

A quick knock sounded on his front door followed by Naomi letting herself in. "I'm back. You both okay?" She hurried to Jack's bed and checked the pulses on both him and Butch.

"We're still here," he replied. "Everything all right at home?"

She grunted as she sat down. "Yes. My all-purpose robot blew a fuse and froze up and couldn't make lunch. My silly grandson was hungry and didn't know how to repair her."

Robots were not as helpful as they were advertised to be, in Jack's opinion. Although he'd had to change with the times throughout the many decades, he had sworn he'd never own a robot. There was nothing wrong with good old fashioned hard work, the way he'd been raised. In fact, he still owned the straw broom Maisie had swept their cabin floor with, and although most of the bristles were gone, it still served its purpose.

"I swear, kids today are so spoiled," Naomi chuckled. She folded her hands in her lap. "I'm ready to hear the rest of your tale. You were about to tell me how you and Butch have…lived so long." Her eyebrow arched with intrigue.

Jack's throat constricted, and he suddenly felt very weak. Poor Butch was breathing erratically, too. They'd be giving up the ghost in no time. He would have to talk fast.

"The miracle happened one summer day back in nineteen eleven when Butch and I were fishing in a hidden cove on Lake Tavadora. One moment he was standing in the rowboat with his front feet on the bow, and the next, he was clamped tight within the jaws of a mammoth gator."

CHAPTER FOUR

Naomi's eyes enlarged. "Oh my!" She cut a glance at the furry lump on Jack's chest. "Obviously, he survived, unless he's a clone."

"He's no clone," Jack assured. "Butch is an original, the one and only."

"What happened?"

"That gator was at least ten feet long with a mouth as wide as a canyon and teeth as sharp as razor blades. The moment Butch was in his mouth, the creature dove into the water and disappeared."

"What'd you do?"

"I threw my fishin' pole aside and dove in after him."

Naomi's jaw dropped. "You didn't!"

"I did." Jack felt blood rush through his veins at the memory. "Adrenaline kicked in, I guess, and there was no thinking, only reacting. I had to save my little buddy."

"But that gator could have attacked you. I'm surprised he didn't."

"Want to know what surprised *me* the most?" Jack asked.

She nodded vigorously.

"It was finding out that Butch can hold his breath for a long time under water. And he's a mighty good swimmer, too. I didn't know either of those things before." He laughed and Naomi joined him.

"As soon as I dove in, I was able to grab a hold of that gator's tail. When I did, he snapped his head around. His jaws opened and Butch swam out of his mouth. My little buddy paddled away from the monster and up to the surface as fast as his paws and legs would carry him. Luckily, the gator let him escape. I guess he figured I'd make for a heartier meal. When he eyed me and shot forward, I made a quick turn in the water and clubbed him in the nose with the heel of my boot."

"Did the kick kill him?"

"No, but it stunned him long enough for me to make my own escape. I was about out of breath by then, so I frantically stroked my way to the surface. Out of the corner of my eye, I saw the beast swim away in the opposite direction. I couldn't believe he was going to let me be, but I was grateful."

Naomi was on the edge of her chair. "When you got to the surface, was your rowboat where you'd left it and was Butch clinging to it?"

"Nope. Strangely, my boat was nowhere to be found, but the sun was bright and the rays bounced off the water like lightning bolts. My head was dizzy from holding my breath so long underwater. Perhaps I just didn't notice the boat in my panic to see if Butch had survived. When I glanced around, I caught sight of a small island I didn't recognize, and there was a little animal standing on the beach. Even though I was about tuckered out, I had no option but to swim toward the island. As I got closer, I realized that drowned rat wagging its tail was Butch!"

"Thank goodness he was alive," Naomi said, as if she didn't already know.

"Yeah, but I was almost done for. Remember, I was sixty-one years old, so that run-in with the gator and the swimming excursion took a lot out of me. Once I dragged myself onto the shore, I collapsed. But I sure was glad to see Butch. He greeted me with a lot of kisses to my face. Although he had teeth wounds on each cheek, surprisingly the cuts weren't deep and he appeared no worse for wear."

Naomi stood up and leaned over to tug the blanket down to peer at the dog's sleeping face.

"Yes, those are the scars," Jack said, referring to the vertical lines on both sides of Butch's face.

"I always wondered how he got those. It's amazing that alligator didn't swallow him whole."

"I don't think he meant to hurt Butch. I think he just wanted to play."

"Play?" Her voice lifted an octave, clearly in disagreement.

"Believe it or not, I discovered later that the old fella was pretty friendly and could be sociable when he wanted to be."

"An alligator sociable? Never heard of such a thing." She rolled her eyes and plopped back onto her chair.

"He showed himself to a few special people through the years and never hurt any of them. He and I even became friends. We respected each other."

"Oh my." She squinted. "Say, aren't you sixty-one years old now?"

"Yes."

"And this incident with the gator happened in nineteen eleven?"

"Yep."

She smiled. "You've held your age well."

"That's certainly been true, until very recently."

"Please go on. I won't interrupt anymore," Naomi said.

Butch suddenly turned onto his side and yelped. "Poor little man. I'm nearing the end of my account, but I'd better hurry. He's fading fast, and so am I." Jack could feel his life blood draining quickly.

"No, Jack, don't say that." Naomi's face twisted as if she were the one in pain.

"The time for the two of us to answer the final summons is long overdue," he replied. She gave him another drink of water and he continued. "That island was one I'd never seen before, so once my energy returned, Butch and I did a little exploring. I thought I'd been to every island and upon every shore Tavadora Lake had to offer, but this was a hidden place, a special place, I came to realize."

"Special, in what way?" Naomi had promised not to interrupt again, but she apparently couldn't help herself.

Jack paused for dramatic effect before whispering, "That's where we found the fountain of youth."

207

Her mouth opened.

"As Butch and I were investigating, I heard what sounded like a waterfall in the distance. We followed the sound, and once we approached, I discovered it wasn't a waterfall at all, but a gushing spring that exited the side of a small hill and filled a stream that fed into the lake. Butch immediately jumped into the stream and paddled around, lapping up the water. I was thirsty after all the excitement myself, so I knelt and drank in several handfuls." He smiled. "That water was the cleanest, freshest, most pure water I'd ever tasted." He licked his lips at remembering.

"Did you feel the miracle happening right then?" Naomi asked.

"No. We walked back to the shore where we'd washed up and, lo and behold, there was my rowboat bobbing in the water. I rowed us home and we went to bed, exhausted from the day. The next morning I got out of bed without suffering a single ache or pain. When I looked in the mirror, my wrinkles were gone, and it seemed my face was more youthful. I certainly felt spry, and there was a kick in my step. Throughout the morning, I noticed my hip didn't hurt when I walked, and I no longer leaned to the side. My back felt straighter. Muscles that had naturally grown weak felt harder under my touch. Even Butch acted like a puppy again. He was yapping and running around, jumping on and off the furniture. Later that afternoon, he and I were back out on the fishing boat doing our usual routine when, suddenly, I felt as old as the hills. At first, I thought it was the sun taking its toll, but inside, I knew that I'd physically regressed since earlier that morning. All the aches and pains returned. Even Butch lost his pep."

"What'd you do?"

"I rowed us back to that secret island. I docked the boat, and we returned to the hidden spring. Butch and I drank our fill from the stream, and by the time we got back home, my body felt like that of a man thirty years younger. Butch bounced off the walls, he had so much energy."

Naomi stared at him wide-eyed. "So, the spring really was the fountain of youth?"

"As far as I was concerned it was. After a few days following the same routine, I knew I'd discovered the secret to eternal life. Something was in that water that caused man and dog alike to stop growing old if drank on a daily basis. Every afternoon from that moment on, Butch and I rowed to that island and indulged in our magic potion, as I liked to call it.

Over time, I figured out how much was required per day to maintain our youthful vitality. Eventually, I began to haul bottles and jugs to the spring. I filled them up and stored them at my house, because there were days when it was inconvenient for me to row to the island. As long as we drank the spring water on a daily basis, Butch and I remained healthy and we never aged another day. This went on for years."

209

After sitting silent for several long moments, Naomi stated the inevitable. "And then the lake dried up."

Jack nodded. "I saw it coming—I'd been blessed with a second sight since birth—so for thirty years I collected water from the source. I stored it in fifty-gallon drums on my property. Butch and I have been drinking what we needed from my supply every day, until just recently."

"And that's because you finally ran out." It was a statement, not a question.

"Yes. Now we're both drying up, just like the lake." Jack chuckled softly at his joke. "I just wanted someone to know how special this town and the lake used to be, before the earth's climate changed and technology took over the world. I've seen and experienced a lot of things, and I have to say, times were better when life was simpler."

"Oh, Jack." Naomi sniffled and squeezed back tears. "After living such a long and full life, are you afraid to...to…?"

"Die?" There was no bitterness in his tone and no hesitation with his answer. "No. I don't look at it as leaving anything behind. Butch and I are moving toward something, or should I say…someone."

Naomi seemed to understand. "Maisie?"

There was a hitch in his voice when he answered. "She's waiting for us on the other side."

As if on cue, what felt like invisible fingers moved over his scalp, down his neck, and raked his shoulders. He stared at a spot on the wall across the room and felt love flowing toward him. Warmth enveloped him. Suddenly, Butch opened his eyes and lifted his head, awareness causing his fur to tingle under Jack's fingertips. Jack scooted him into the crook of his arm, and the dog's gaze also shifted to the wall.

Taking notice of the change in their behavior, Naomi looked in that direction. "Jack? What do you see? Is it your wife?"

A light, brighter than any he'd ever seen blinded him. Music, more beautiful than any worldly music, filled his ears. Butch's ears perked. The dog gingerly licked his face, appearing more alive than he had for the past few hours.

As if his body were set on a timer, Jack suddenly felt his organs shutting down, one after the other. Although he could have been frightened, or at least curious as to what it meant to live eternally in a different realm, he wasn't. There was no discomfort at all, only thankfulness, love, and anticipation.

So this is it, he thought. *It's finally time to meet my Maker*. He placed his hand over Butch's slow-beating heart. Inside his own chest he could feel his ticker's sluggish rhythm. He closed his eyes.

His jaw tightened, and the blood running through his veins slowed to a crawl, causing him to feel as if he were floating. In fact, he suddenly found himself above the room looking down at his body lying in the bed. He watched as Naomi gently jiggled his arm and spoke his name several times.

Although he opened his mouth, he was no longer able to speak. She had been a good friend to the end. He regretted not being able to tell her how much he appreciated her kindness and care, but the words simply would not come.

She clapped a hand over her mouth. Her chest heaved, and tears began to slide down her cheeks. She grabbed his hand. "This is it, isn't it?" She didn't wait for an answer, because she knew none would come. "Goodbye, my dear, sweet friend. I wish you and Butch a safe journey."

From his viewpoint on the bedroom ceiling, Jack turned his head to see Butch hovering next to him. He spoke to him through his mind. "*It's time for us to go to the big lake in the sky, little man.*"

Butch yipped in a voice only Jack could hear. He swept the dog into his arms and held tight as memories of his 270 years on earth flashed through his mind like a motion picture.

Featured in his reel of life was everyone who had meant so much to him—his parents, his baby brother, good friends like Jennie Sullivan, Casey and Joe Walden, and Tad Singer. With lips curved into a grin, Jack silently thanked them all for their love and companionship.

A sweet and familiar voice whispered in his ear, "*Come home. I'm waiting.*"

Smiling, he replied, "We're on our way, Maisie."

Then Jack released a final shudder, and together man and dog began their new journey.

About the Author

Stacey Coverstone is a multi-published author in a variety of genres. All of her books are available digitally and many can be found in paperback. She is also a fiction editor. If you are a writer looking for an editor to help polish your book for publication, please visit the Editing Services page of her website. She likes working with both new and more established authors.

Stacey lives in the beautiful lakeside town of Mount Dora, Florida with her husband and their long-haired German Shepherd. In her spare time, she enjoys the many outdoor activities Florida has to offer, reading, motorcycle and bicycle riding, photography, target shooting, traveling, and making scrapbooks of her adventures.

Aside from writing and editing, Stacey also has a day job, working in Sales and Catering at the charming and historic (and some say *haunted*) 1883 Lakeside Inn.

Although the author has taken creative liberty with some aspects of the setting, Mount Dora, Lake Dora, and the Lakeside Inn were the inspiration for this book.

Please visit Stacey's website for information on all of her romantic, mysterious, and paranormal novels, novellas, and short stories. www.staceycoverstone.com

If you enjoyed this book, please consider posting a short review on Amazon. It's an easy way to champion a book and let other readers know you liked the author's work. Thank you!

75278140R00121

Made in the USA
Columbia, SC
16 August 2017